THE
RADICAL RADIANCE
OF THE
FISHING FLY

A NOVEL

LEWIS K. SCHRAGER

LFEA
PRESS

ABOUT THE AUTHOR

Lewis K. Schrager is an author and playwright whose short stories have twice earned honors in the F. Scott Fitzgerald Literary Contest.

His work has appeared in *South Carolina Review*, *Cottonwood, Bryant Literary Review, Colere, Quiddity, South Dakota Review, Southwestern American Literature, Talking River*, and *Windhover*.

His plays, *Levy's Ghost, Shadow of the Valley*, and *Fourteen Days in July*, have been produced in Baltimore, Maryland, and St. Paul, Minnesota.

The Radical Radiance of the Fishing Fly is his first published novel.

A graduate of Johns Hopkins University and the Vanderbilt University School of Medicine, Schrager earned his Master's in Writing (fiction concentration) from Johns Hopkins in 2003. In addition to his literary career, he has dedicated much of his professional life to advancing global health, serving as an HIV/AIDS researcher at the U.S. National Institutes of Health and as a vaccine developer focused on tuberculosis prevention.

Schrager lives in North Bethesda, Maryland, with his wife, Frances Marshall.

Library of Congress Control Number: 2025907636

ISBN 979-8-9927199-0-1 (paperback)
ISBN 979-8-9927199-1-8 (epub)

Printed in the United States of America

Book Design by Amy Lynn Foster
Cover photo by Amy Lynn Foster
Additional cover elements from a photo by Marcelo Matarazzo on Unsplash
Author photo by Elana Schrager

This is a work of fiction. Names, characters, organizations, and incidents either are products
of the author's imagination or are used fictitiously.

For Ralph
Your love, laughter, passion, and friendship
Forever will be missed

THE
RADICAL
RADIANCE
OF THE
FISHING FLY

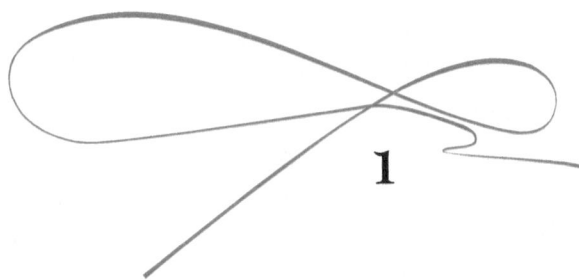

1

I pulled out of the underground garage onto Wisconsin Avenue, then down the ramp heading east on the Washington Beltway. Rays of the rising sun glowed orange in a far-off bank of clouds. Gray banks of night fog, exhaled from dying creeks and streams entrapped within the urban sprawl, drifted over the roadway bridges before dissipating as rising haze over the slim remains of vestigial marshland. I turned onto I-95 North, speeding past countless semis parked close along the shoulders of the highway, red running lights blinking crazy in the half-light. I imagined the truckers awakening in their dark, coffin-like spaces, yawning and stretching and rubbing their eyes as they plan for another day bringing who-knows-what to who-knows-where.

Wondering where I was going.

Wondering why.

In fact, I knew. My destination on that steamy August morning was the Philadelphia airport, a rendezvous with my older brother Larry. In less than three hours I would be meeting him there. We would board our plane to Seattle, and then another to Anchorage, and then a third and a fourth, our destination somewhere in the Alaskan wilderness for a week of fly fishing.

The first rays of the freshly risen sun flared above the distant cloudbank. I squinted against the blinding glare, lowered my sun visor, fumbled with my sunglasses, and slipped them on.

This was a bad idea.

I was nervous about spending this much time with Larry. Growing up, he was brash and loud, determined to be the center of attention. I was quiet, more than happy to disappear into the background, unnoticed and undisturbed. This worked out fine when we were apart. On the few occasions where we found ourselves thrown together, like at an occasional high school party, he'd notice my subtle signals of embarrassment at his behavior and would talk more loudly, act more wildly, dance more crazily, until I shrunk away into a kind of nothingness and headed home on my own. I could never even think of taking him on physically when he pushed me past my breaking point as he was taller and far stronger than I, and a champion wrestler as well.

I tried to convince myself that this fishing trip would work out fine. So much had changed since our high school days. Larry had become a successful businessman, having grown *Leather and More*, our father's store in South Philly to three times its original size. He'd expanded the business, establishing a second store in the Mall at Short Hills, a prime shopping destination in the tony New Jersey suburbs just west of New York City. He'd married Tina Simons, a wonderful woman who gave him a couple of lovely daughters. He'd mellowed.

Besides, I realized that all this cogitation was irrelevant. Mellowed or not, I never would have agreed to go on this trip if not for Larry's cancer.

Although I'm a doctor by training, I had long ago left the rigors of dealing with the sick and dying in favor of a research position at the National Institutes of Health. Even so, members of my family call on me when medical questions arise. I still remember Tina's call on a cold, gray morning in November two years before. Larry had been coughing badly but had ignored her pleas to get checked out. He assured her that it was nothing, just a cold. It would get better with time. It didn't—in fact, his coughing grew worse—and she called me. Larry took the phone from her. He began to brag about how badly the Eagles were going to crush the Redskins in the game on tap for later that day (as if I really cared)—and then started coughing. I'd heard that kind of cough before; hard and dry, sounding like his body was trying to expel his lungs from his chest. "You sound like shit," I said.

"It's just a ..." His spasm of coughing was long enough for me to pace twice around my bedroom before it quieted.

"Just a cold? Sounds like a bad one to me. You sure you don't have TB or something?"

"Funny, that's what Tina said."

"Well, do you?"

"Hell no," he said. "Besides, they already put one of those TB skin tests on me."

"So?"

"They said it was negative."

"When?"

"A couple of weeks ago," he said.

"A couple of weeks? You've been coughing like this for a couple of goddamned weeks?"

"Longer. They did the test a couple of weeks ago."

"Did they check you for whooping cough?"

"Whooping? Does it sound like I'm whooping? Jesus, I'm just coughing."

"Sometimes adults with whooping cough don't whoop," I said. "Did they check you?"

"I have no fucking idea."

"What about a chest X-ray?"

"I don't need any ..."

His lungs exploded once again. I waited, my free hand balled into a tight fist, until the coughing abated. "Hate to clue you, Larry, but you can barely breathe. If you came to the NIH, they wouldn't let you in without a mask."

"Lucky I'm not coming to the NIH. Never did, probably never fucking will." I held the phone away from myself, squeezing it tight, wondering why it always seemed to get like this. "You still there?" I heard him say in the arm's-length distance between the phone and my ear.

I closed my eyes and brought the phone closer. "Still here," I said.

"You know how much I hate hospitals," Larry said in that way that let me know that he'd gone too far and was sorry for it.

"Yeah, I know. I'll find you a pulmonary specialist," I said. "Meanwhile, make sure you get an X-ray. Promise me."

"Yeah, sure," he said in that way that I knew he had no intention of doing it.

Not too long after, the glands in his neck began to swell. Then the chills and fevers started, mostly at night, followed by sweats that soaked his bedclothes and sheets. Tina's threat to sleep in the guest room finally convinced him to get an X-ray and an appointment with the pulmonary specialist I'd found for him.

I read the film minutes after it was taken, the image sent to me electronically at the NIH by prearrangement with Dr. Joanna Ramanathan, assistant chief of pulmonology at the University of Pennsylvania Hospital, and a former medical school classmate of mine. I was staring at it on the computer screen when Joanna called me. "It's not good, David," she said. Even in medical school, Joanna always had trouble suppressing her emotions in the way that doctors are trained to do; one of the reasons, I believe, that all her patients seemed to love her. I could imagine the tears gathering in her dark eyes.

"It'll be lucky if it's TB," I said as if making just another casual observation on some new patient's X-ray, sparing Joanna the need to say what I knew she was thinking.

A biopsy of one of Larry's swollen neck glands confirmed what Joanna and I had suspected: Larry had developed Hodgkin's lymphoma. Scans showed that the cancer had spread throughout his body. His fevers and night sweats worsened the prognosis. Despite all this bad news, I also understood that, if you had to develop cancer, things could be a lot worse than getting Hodgkin's. The cancer was curable with radiation and chemotherapy; I took some solace in that.

After a year of radiation treatments to his neck and chest and three-week cycles of chemo, the oncologist declared Larry cancer-free.

His remission only lasted three months. The return of the cancer meant that bone marrow transplantation was the only hope for saving him.

The fevers, chills, and sweats that soaked his pajamas and bedsheets began on the eighth day after the transplantation, when his immune system had been wiped out by the high-dose chemotherapy. From one visit to the next I could see him fade before my eyes, his face turning sallow and skeleton-like, barely recognizable. Even with my medical training, it was hard to watch; hard, also, to see Tina's mask of steely, stoic optimism she displayed inside the hospital melt beneath an uncontrollable flow of tears when out of Larry's sight.

Larry, however, didn't suffer through these nearly unbearable discomforts while lying prone and helpless in bed. Throughout all but the worst days of his ordeal, he spent most of his waking hours sitting in a hard-backed chair facing the narrow window of his sealed-off room. He used his bedside table as his workbench, the top strewn with spools of black thread and silver fishhooks alongside a wooden box with thirty or so smaller boxes inside, each containing beads, hairs, feathers, tinsel, cotton, and bits and pieces of wood, wire, and plastic. His fingers deftly selected pieces of this multicolored mélange to include in his next creation intended to mimic the appearance of salmon eggs, orange wiggle tail flies, polar shrimp, egg-sucking leeches, even baby gray mice—an array of fishing flies chosen for their ability to entice fish native to one specific place: the frigid rivers of Alaska.

I found it difficult to concentrate on my work over the ensuing couple of weeks. I run a good-sized lab at the NIH, studying the mechanisms by which cells die, an area of investigation thought arcane by many, except for those who understand its relevance to fighting cancer. Diving back into my lab work only seemed to bring Larry's struggle into sharper focus. A routine gaze through my microscope at the immune cells on which I work instantly brought to mind Larry's lymphoma. I stared at the cells, wondering why he'd waited so long to get his cough checked out, why he took so long to call me. Even when the call came, it was from Tina, not him. But that's the way it always was, a distance between us reaching back into childhood that I couldn't narrow or even begin to understand.

I returned to the hospital on the day of Larry's discharge,

after his marrow had engrafted and repopulated his body with new, healthy, infection-fighting immune cells. His cancer appeared to be gone. I arrived just as Larry was getting dressed. Tina greeted me with a hug that squeezed the wind out of me, a *thank God* look in her eyes. It hit me that I was inside his room without a mask covering my face. "Nice to be free from all those tubes," Larry said as he finished buttoning his red-and-black plaid flannel shirt. He picked a box off the bedside table and handed it to me. "Check this out, bro," he said.

This was a bigger box than the one containing the beads and baubles, its compartments spilling over with fishing flies. Beaded eyes peered from cottony heads, delicate feathered wings amongst a jumbled swarm of dragonfly nymphs so lifelike as to make you want to slap your hand over the top of the compartment to prevent their escape, miniature gray mice looking forlorn in their entrapment. I picked out one of the mice and gently bounced it in my open palm, the point of the expertly hidden hook sharp on my skin. "You did all this?" I said.

"Two hundred and nineteen, but who's counting?"

"That should catch you a lot of fish," I said.

"Catch *us* a lot of fish." He glanced at Tina. She smiled in that way that people do when sharing a secret.

"He wants you to go, too," Tina said. "I think it's a great idea."

I looked away for a moment, my eyes focused on a poster he'd taped on the wall behind his bed, curtain-like folds of the aurora borealis glowing green in the night sky above a moonlit winter vista. Our mother used to talk about seeing the northern lights during a vacation she had taken long ago with her family up in Canada. Our father had promised that he would take us all back to Canada to see the lights someday, a promise forgotten after cancer took our mother at far too young an age.

"You game?" Larry said.

I wasn't. Not in the least.

"Sure," I said, feeling as if my response came from a ventriloquist hidden somewhere in the room.

"Okay!" Larry said and slapped me a palm-stinging high five. "I'm looking at the second week in August. The bugs are pretty much played out, the days are still long but it's dark enough to sleep at night, the weather is cool but not freezing cold, and the snows haven't begun yet."

And now, on this steamy morning of the first day of the second week of August, I pulled into the long-term lot at the Philadelphia International Airport, boarded a shuttle for the terminal, and took my place at the end of the long, snaking line outside the Southwest ticket counter, my duffel bag at my feet, searching the faces for him.

Larry had sent me a list of things to pack, scanned in from a letter he'd received from the leader of the trip, some guy named Wiley Williams. I followed the list as precisely as I could, packing much lighter than I wanted to. I didn't have much choice given the note written in bold caps across the bottom of the letter: **EVERYTHING YOU BRING WILL BE HAND-CHECKED BY ME AND MUST FIT INTO A SINGLE WATERPROOF BAG I WILL SUPPLY. IF IT DOESN'T FIT, IT SITS—NO EXCEPTIONS!** Larry said that Wiley Williams was the best Alaskan back-country fishing guide out there, that we were unbelievably lucky to book spots with him. I read that note, hoping that he was a nicer guy in person than he sounded in his letter.

The only thing missing from my bag was fishing gear. Waders, waterproof fly-fishing boots, a fly rod, line, and flies—Larry said he had extras and would take care of all this for me. The fit wasn't going to be perfect—his feet were about a size bigger than mine—but for a week, he figured they'd do.

"Hey, David," Larry's voice boomed out from behind me. He dropped his duffel bag at my feet and engulfed me in his arms. "Good to see you, bro. This is going to be a blast!"

"I hope so," I said and glanced down at his duffel. "I thought we needed to pack light."

"Half of it's for you." He unzipped his bag and handed me chest waders, a fishing vest, boots, and a bunch of other waterproof gear, along with a phallic-looking leather case containing a disarticulated fly rod and reel. I crammed it all inside my bag. "If it gets wet and cold, you gotta have the right gear."

"I thought it doesn't get wet and cold in August. Isn't that why we're going now?"

"We're less likely to have nasty weather now, but you never can tell. Probabilities, bro; you're the hot-shot scientist." I always hated when he called me that. "I'm looking out for you, kiddo. I don't want you worrying about anything."

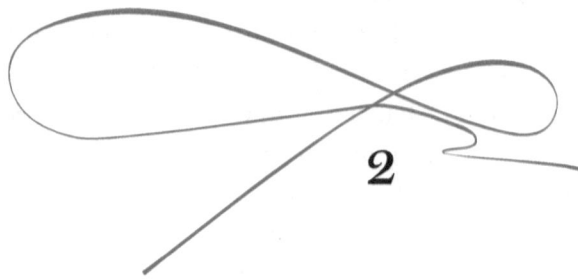

2

Larry took the window seat straight through to Anchorage. I didn't fight it. I knew that he'd enjoy seeing the Mississippi, the geometric quilt of farms on the plains, the snow-capped Rockies. I bargained for the window seat on the return flight, figuring that I'd probably be exhausted by then and could sleep against the side of the plane.

We didn't talk a whole lot on the long ride out, but that was fine. Larry disappeared into the movies on the tiny display built into the back of the seats in front of us. He coaxed me into watching an *Avengers* flick, but I soon grew tired of it. After about half an hour, I began to read a grant proposal I'd stashed into my backpack. Larry nudged me with his elbow. "Best seller?" he said.

"Not exactly." He gave me a look like I was hopeless and returned to his movie. I returned to the document, a proposal from a team at MIT's Whitehead Institute seeking an additional five years of support for their research into a new enzyme, which they hypothesized played a critical role in mediating the programmed cell death pathway in T-cells.

Larry tapped me on my shoulder. "I hope you're not planning on spending this vacation doing work."

"I'm putting it all away when we land in Anchorage. Promise."

Larry readjusted his headphones and settled back into his seat. Normally I'm annoyed when a stranger sitting next to me on a plane laughs out loud while watching an in-flight movie. This time I didn't mind given all he'd been through. At some point Larry dozed off. With his head turned away from me, the cold blue light from the screen illuminated the scars on his neck, a tortured map of the lymph node biopsies his doctors had used to check the progress of his treatment. One scar had become infected, looking like skin that had been seared with a branding iron. For a moment, I thought of him as a boy, his skin smooth and whole, his body unmarred by the poisonous chemicals and toxic radiation, which along with his bone marrow transplantation, had saved him from the cancer.

It was about 8 p.m. in Anchorage but 2 a.m. back East by the time our bags came through. Waiting in the line for the hotel shuttle, I sensed the full extent of my exhaustion. "That's it," Larry said, and nudged me toward an approaching van, *Osprey Inn* scrawling in yellow dot letters across the sign above the windshield. I climbed in, tossed my bags on the luggage rack, and collapsed into a window seat near the back. Larry sat down next to me.

The van turned a tight corner and pulled into the second section of the terminal. I had almost dozed off when Larry elbowed me in my ribs. "Holy shit, check it out!" Larry whispered. "Goddamn if it ain't Tyler Babcock!"

A big fellow with a walrus-like mustache headed toward us, followed by a trim, clean-shaven companion.

"Who's Tyler Babcock?" I whispered.

Larry gave me a look like I was denser than lead. "Seriously?" he whispered. "Only the most famous fisherman in the whole goddamn country. Got his own show on the Fishing Channel!"

Babcock and friend took seats across the aisle from us. I closed my eyes as we pulled away from the terminal, my head knocking against the window.

"Mr. *Babcock*?" Larry said. He sounded breathless. Awe-struck.

"Yep."

"Love your show. Watch it all the time."

"Glad to hear it. You plannin' on doin' some fishin'?"

"That's why I came. Heading out tomorrow."

"Me, too. Where you goin'?"

"Nalunaq, wherever the hell that is. Leaving from there to do some back-country fishing."

"I'll be damned, so am I."

"You serious? You wouldn't be going with Wiley Williams?"

"That's just who I'm goin' with! Heard that Wiley knows the Alaskan back country like nobody else. Figured I'd check him out, maybe give him some airtime on one of my shows next year. Be good for his business."

I could just about hear Larry's heart pounding inside his chest. "We're on the same goddamned trip!" he gasped.

"Looks like it," Tyler Babcock said. "You here by yourself?"

"Nope, traveling with my brother." He nudged me with his elbow, jarring me back into full consciousness. "I'm Larry. This here's David."

Tyler Babcock shook Larry's hand and then mine; his hand big, strong, and sandpaper rough. Babcock turned to the smaller man in the window seat alongside of him. "Tony, this is Larry and David," he said. "They're on Wiley's trip." Tony leaned forward and offered a salute before settling back into his seat. "Tony's my assistant producer, goes with me when I travel. You a fisherman, too?" Babcock asked me.

"Not yet," Larry said. "But we'll make him one."

"Can't force fishin' on nobody," Babcock said. "It's like anything else, I guess; you're either into it or you ain't. To some folks, it's the most boring thing in the world, spending your God-given days tossing a string in the water, hoping some goddamned fish will latch on so you can reel her in and then throw her back. To be totally honest, sometimes I see their point. Of course I love it, or I wouldn't be spending my life doin' it." Babcock smiled, big white teeth beneath his mustache, and the thought came to me that I might come to like this guy. "So, David, if you ain't a fisherman, why you comin' along on this trip—if you don't mind me askin'?"

"Larry invited me," I said. "I always wanted to see Alaska, so I figured, why not?"

"But you never fished before."

"Actually, I once went fishing for blues off the Jersey shore with my dad and Larry," I said before I remembered why I shouldn't have said it.

"Yeah, so how'd that go?"

"Not great," I said. "I got seasick."

"He puked all over the deck," Larry said.

Babcock smiled. "Tell you what, I got seasick myself the first time I went deep sea fishin'," he said. "That's why I stuck to rivers and lakes the rest of my life. Don't you worry, you ain't gettin' seasick on this trip. Your ass'll get tired from the sitting, you may get cold and wet depending on the weather, but no way you're gettin' seasick. Sounds like a pretty shitty trip you had there."

Shitty trip was right. After that, there was no way that this fishing trip could be any worse, I figured. No way at all.

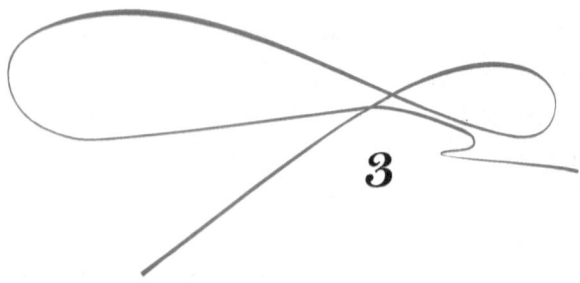

3

Babcock asked me and Larry to join him and some others going on Wiley's trip for dinner in town. I went along, even though I could barely keep my eyes open. We headed over to a place called Koots. The saloon looked like a survivor from Gold Rush days: all timber, our footsteps leaving tracks in the sawdust on the floor like we were walking through dirty snow. It was big and loud, filled with burly, bearded men and large, busty women shouting to each other over the background noise, laughing big, loud laughs, slamming thick-bottomed glasses down on scarred wooden tabletops.

A big guy with a shaved head and a fire-red beard jumped up from his seat as we passed. "Holy shit, it's Tyler fuckin' Babcock!" he shouted and threw his arms around Babcock in a back-pounding man-hug. Babcock grinned and engaged the fellow in some small talk before pulling a Sharpie from the front pocket of his jeans and signing his name across the shoulders of his fan's Z-Z Top T-shirt.

Babcock sat down in the middle of a long table in a back corner of the room. The others in our party hustled to fill the seats in close to him like he was Jesus Christ settling in for the Last Supper. Tony sat on Babcock's left; Larry snatched the seat immediately to his right. Three fishing buddies from Nashville—Carl Cooper, Paul Acer, and Tommy Ewing—grabbed the seats directly across from him. I sat at the far end of the table alongside a barrel-chested, red-faced car salesman from Oklahoma City named Russ McPherson. Russ told me that he and Bob Billings, his insurance agent friend sitting alongside of him, had been saving money for five years to take this trip. I barely had the chance to tell him my name before he seemed to stop breathing. His face went from red to deep purple, his eyes bulging. He pulled a handkerchief out of his back pants pocket and loosed a long, wheezy cough into the wrinkled cloth. I wondered what the hell he was thinking, heading off into the Alaskan wilderness for a week of fishing and camping with lungs that bad, hundreds of miles from the nearest hospital.

With all the noise, I could only catch bits and pieces of the fish-speak flying around the table; talk of babines and orange wiggle tails, tippets and nail knots, some vaguely familiar from conversations with Larry, but most of it sounding like comic gibberish to me. Everyone seemed to be speaking to Tyler Babcock, seeking tidbits of wisdom, telling stories to impress. No one seemed more vocal than Larry, his eyes as happy as I'd seen them for as long as I could remember.

I awoke the next morning to the beeping of Larry's watch alarm. After a quick breakfast of a hard-boiled egg, blueberry Dannon yogurt, a banana, and Lipton tea in a Styrofoam cup, I followed Larry, Babcock, and the others, including a narrow-faced guy who hadn't been at last night's dinner, through a thick, chilly fog into the airport shuttle van. The dour-looking stranger found a seat by himself in the back of the van. I glanced back at him as I sat down, hoping that he wasn't part of Wiley's group.

Babcock stroked his mustache as he gazed out his window. "We ain't going nowhere until this fog lifts," he murmured to himself.

We were booked on an 8 a.m. flight to Nalunaq, a village in west-central Alaska on the junction of the Kuskokwim and Nalunaq Rivers. We followed Babcock through the terminal to the Air Denali ticketing desk, the silent stranger following at a distance. A groan rose from the group when we learned that our flight was delayed. "The fog's going to lift, boys," Babcock said. "We've just got to be a little patient."

"The fog around here isn't the problem," the young fellow working behind the desk said to Babcock. "It's worse out in Nalunaq."

"So, when do you think we're getting out of here?" Babcock said.

"Can't say. Only two planes heading to Nalunaq today. You guys are in the first. There's a hunting party going out on the 3:30."

You could see the relief on Babcock's face. "So, the first plane's just for us? Shit, that means we can go out any time."

"Not exactly. After four hours, our pilots go home. It's in their contract."

"You gotta be shitting me," Babcock said.

"Actually, I'm not."

"Then when the hell are we leaving for Nalunaq?"

The young man behind the counter fidgeted with his pen. "Can't exactly tell you," he said.

I glanced at the Air Denali agent's nametag—*Tom Bowens*. "So, Tom," I said, "Could we get on the second plane?"

Tom stared at me as if I'd asked for admission to the Emerald City. "The 3:30?" he said. "Well, I don't know—"

"The 3:30 will work for us," Babcock said. "It'll get us in later than Wiley was expecting, but it'd be a hell of a lot better than getting stuck here until Sunday."

"Sunday?" Tom Bowens said. "You mean Monday."

Babcock leaned in toward Tom Bowens like he hadn't heard right. "This here's Saturday morning. That means tomorrow's Sunday, and if we get stuck here today, we fly the hell out of here tomorrow. Sunday. *Capice?*"

"Unfortunately, sir, the Nalunaq airport is closed to commercial air traffic on Sunday. After the afternoon flight, the next plane out is at 8:30 Monday morning."

Babcock laid his two big hands flat on the counter, his head bowed between his arms. "Holy shit in a bucket," he whispered. "This trip's fucked."

"Like hell it is!" Larry said. He pushed past me and leaned over the counter. "We're not letting this trip go down the toilet because of your goddamned airline!" he shouted at Tom. "You figure out a way to get us the hell out of here!"

I took hold of Larry's shoulder, half-turned him away from a wide-eyed Tom Bowens and leaned in close. "It's not his fault," I whispered. "Yelling at him will make things worse."

"Worse? What's worse than getting stuck in fucking Anchorage and watching this trip go straight to hell?"

"How about ending up in jail for harassing an airport employee? Just chill for a second." I turned back to Tom. "Tell me about the 3:30 flight," I said.

Tom took a deep breath and pulled a clipboard from beneath the counter. He scanned the piece of paper fastened to it, then counted our group silently with a pointed finger. "Ten. You might be in luck. Our turboprops seat fifteen, but we don't usually fly them full what with the headwind heading west unless we have to. Looks like we've got five booked on the late flight."

"The hunters," I said.

"Right. Your gear may be a problem, with all the weight."

"Our gear's not going to be a problem," Babcock said. "A five-seater's taking us out to the back country tomorrow, we had to pack light."

"Okay, I'll put you down for the 3:30. Let's hope it's not necessary."

I spent the rest of the morning staring out the big window at the fog-shrouded runway. At a little before noon the world outside began to brighten; I walked to the window, looked up and spied the sun, pale and moonlike through the thinning clouds. I went to the desk and asked Celia, who had taken over for Tom during his lunch break, about the chances of our getting out before the 12:30 p.m. deadline. "I'm sorry but that's not going to happen," she said, fidgeting with the end of the thick braid of black hair draped over her shoulder. "Nalunaq is still socked in. Right now, you boys will be lucky if the 3:30 flies."

I was going to give Babcock and the others the bad news but decided against it. It looked like Babcock already had given up on the earlier flight. Tony had arranged some plastic chairs into a semicircle. Babcock sat facing the other fishermen, beginning where he'd left off the night before at Koot's, regaling Larry and the others with stories of fly-fishing expeditions from New York to New Zealand, Chile to China. I thought about returning to that MIT grant proposal but couldn't bring myself to open it, distracted by Babcock's story of his trip down the steaming Amazon, the mosquitoes thick enough to block his sight through the netting over his face.

"I thought I'd seen everything until the first time a peacock bass hit my fly," Babcock said, his voice rumbling up from the back of his throat. "That sucker just *exploded* from the river! Damn near pulled the rod right out of my hand. Fought it for more than an hour. When I finally brought it in alongside the boat, I looked down into the dark green water and saw that fish staring up at me with big ole' red eyes. Mean eyes. Devil eyes. Eyes full of hate. I didn't know whether to cut it loose, or bring it on board and bash its goddamn head in."

"So, what did you do?" Larry said.

Babcock sat back and looked out the window at the cloud-filled sky. "Boys, you ain't going to believe this, but I never got the chance to make that decision. I had one hand on my rod, and I was leaning out the boat with my other hand on the line, and suddenly—BLAM!—something comes along and takes my prize bass deep down into the river, and my rod with it."

"Alligator?" Russ guessed.

"Nope."

"Piranha?" Larry asked.

"Try again."

"Well, it wasn't no hippopotamus or he would've taken you and the boat with him," Russ said.

Babcock looked hard at each of the men sitting around him, eventually meeting my own eyes with a stare suggesting that he had seen a vision of the end of the world in that endless flow of water. "Chafalote," he said through his teeth. "Goddamn Chafalote."

"Chafalote?" Russ said. "What the hell's a Chafalote?"

"*Rhaphidon vulpinus*, my friend. The vampire fish." He spread his weathered hands about four feet apart, twisting one way and the other in his seat so everyone around him could see. "Imagine a king salmon about this big," he said. "Now picture that salmon with a mouth full of teeth—big, razor-sharp teeth—and then two fangs, each about five inches long, sticking up from its bottom jaw. That's a Chafalote. Never saw anything like it before, and I pray to God that I never see anything like it again."

The story left the men sitting in breathless silence. It got me wondering what business he had being out on the Amazon in the first place, trespassing upon that endless flow of water born before God had granted humans dominance over all the earth—or before humans had created God as the imagined source of, and justification for, their own dominance. An unholy business, the devil fish taken by the vampire fish. These were my thoughts as I digested Babcock's story. These, I imagined, might be the profound, solemn thoughts of the others as they sat, silent and frozen, their eyes set hard upon Babcock. As would be the case many times on this trip, I was mistaken.

"You ever get your rod back?" Russ asked. Babcock looked square at him, then leaned back with his big arms up and behind him, his fingers intertwined, his head cushioned in the pocket of his joined hands, smiling.

I volunteered to stay behind and watch the bags as most of the group headed off to find something to eat. Only the dour-faced fellow remained behind, sitting alone across the room. I read some of the grant proposal and then thought about pulling out the copy of John McPhee's *Coming into the Country* that I'd brought with me, but I was too tired to do any more reading. I rested my feet up on my bag, struggling to keep my eyes open given my responsibility as watchman—God help me if someone's bag with all their precious fly-fishing gear was pilfered just before heading out on their trip of a lifetime.

I decided to keep myself awake by writing. I pulled my notepad and pen from the front pocket of my jeans and began page one of the chronicle of my journey. Not too long after, Babcock and the fishermen returned, aromas of hamburger and fries drifting from grease-stained paper bags. "Decent burger place down toward baggage claim," Babcock said as he eased himself into one of the hard-backed plastic chairs, a tight fit for him. I thanked him for the suggestion, but my stomach was feeling a little queasy, so I stayed put.

The conversation again turned to the subject of fishing flies. On Babcock's suggestion, the fishermen removed their boxes of flies from their luggage for his inspection. One by one, Babcock set each box on his expansive lap, carefully lifting open the tops as if each had the potential of holding the Crown Jewels. Most of the time, he just looked, nodded in general if not enthusiastic approval, clicked the top shut and passed it back to its owner.

And then he opened Larry's box.

Babcock paused, staring down into the checkerboard of smaller square boxes, each filled with a type of fly Larry had tied during the dangerous days of his bone marrow transplantation. He reached his thick thumb and forefinger into one of the compartments and plucked one out. He held onto the tiny eyelet through which the fishing line would be tied and raised it above his head. Gossamer wings, tiny red eyes, shiny curved tail branching into two spines alongside the curve of the hook seemed to come alive in the blue fluorescence of the ceiling lights, the impaled insect appearing ready to take flight. He set the fly back into its box, lifted another, and another, and another, rotating each one closely before the sharp scrutiny of his narrowed eyes as a jeweler might to a freshly cut diamond, sharing no words, the only expression of his sentiments coming as sudden, small inhalations, barely audible gasps that fluttered the edge of his thick mustache. Babcock studied one for a particularly long time, a tiny sculpture in gray fluff and yarn of a baby mouse masterfully concealing all but the tip of a barbless hook. He set it back into Larry's box, closed the top and fixed a reverent stare upon it while tapping his fingers on the lacquered wooden sides. "How did you do this?" he said without looking up. "How the hell did you manage to do all this?"

I imagined Larry in his isolation room, silhouetted against the winter gray filtering in from the narrow window in front of him, plastic tubes running up the sleeves of his hospital gown, appearing as a life-sized marionette bent over his work bench. I imagined him steadying his hands against the sudden shaking that would presage another fever spike, struggling to force each swallow of his own saliva down his thrush-coated throat. He tied each fly with little else than his own survival at stake, with each new creation a promise to himself of its eventual use in a place wild, open, and free. *That's how he goddamned did it*, I thought.

Larry shrugged his shoulders at the question. I think he may have smiled, but I couldn't really tell.

At just after 2 p.m., Tom, long since back from his lunch break, stepped out from behind the counter. "Might as well line you up now for the 3:30," he called out. "Let's get you weighed before the hunters get here."

"Weighed?" I said.

"It's a small plane," Russ said. "He's got to get us spaced out right, make sure it don't tip over." I waited for a laugh, maybe a slap on my back, some kind of sign that he was kidding. From the look on his face, I could see he wasn't.

We formed a line before a scale big enough to weigh cattle, the metal plate set into the floor, the read-out on the wall-mounted face reaching up to five hundred pounds. I took hold of my duffel and was among the first to step onto the scale. I stood aside and watched as the long black needle marked the weights of the other fishermen, Tom jotting the information down on the paper attached to his clipboard. It all seemed routine until Babcock stepped forward, his brown duffel bag clutched to his chest. The needle shot past two hundred, two-fifty, three hundred, finally reaching a trembling stop at three hundred seventeen pounds. Tom gave him a look like he'd sinned against God and nature. He wrote down some extra notes before asking if anyone else was going to Nalunaq. The dour-faced fellow crossed the room, his duffel thrown over his shoulder, and stepped onto the scale. It had seemed obvious that he'd be joining us, but still I'd hoped that, somehow, he wouldn't. Now, there was no denying it. It would be fine, I told myself. If he became a problem, Wiley Williams would deal with him, I figured.

As we headed back to our seats, I recalled the material that Wiley had sent to us, noting that we'd be traveling in three rafts, each holding four fishermen in addition to a guide. I counted heads; there were only ten of us gathered in the terminal, two were missing from the group. I pointed this out to Larry. "Probably cancelled out," he said. "Too bad for them; no refunds on this trip."

Too bad for them—but the thought that we were here, that

after everything Larry had been through, we really were here, brought a smile to my face.

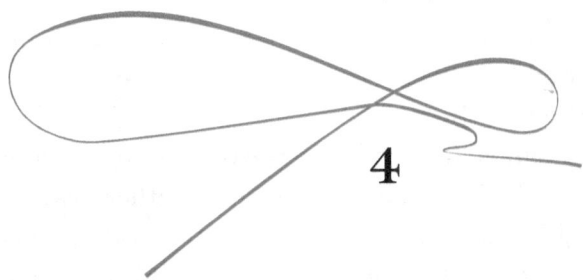

4

Loud voices approaching the waiting area roused me from an unsettling half-sleep. Five men dressed in bulky camouflage hunting suits swaggered by, long-barreled rifles in camo-colored sleeves and heavy-looking, tightly packed duffels dangling from straps over their shoulders. Two of them grasped the extended handles of red plastic coolers, each nearly the size of a park bench, struggling to keep the duffel and gun straps from slipping as they hauled the coolers toward the counter.

Tom directed them to weigh the first cooler, bottles clinking inside as one of the hunters dragged it onto the scale. Tom stared wide-eyed at the needle as it settled in north of ninety pounds. The second cooler was five pounds heavier. *No way in hell Tom's letting those coolers on the plane*, I thought.

Tom jotted down some notes and was about to say something when the leader of the group, a guy they called T.J., stepped forward. He stretched his arm over Tom's shoulders and turned him away from us. I watched in slack-jawed silence as T.J. pulled a wad of cash from his coat pocket, peeled off some bills, and reached for Tom's pants pocket. Tom caught T.J.'s wrist and stopped him. T.J. whispered something in his ear. Tom shot T.J. a worried look, seemed to think for a moment, and then whispered something back. T.J. counted off three more bills and slipped the cash into a front pocket of Tom's pants.

Tom grouped us together in the back of the plane, assigning Babcock, Russ and a couple of the other heavy guys to the single seats on the right. The hunters sat up front. The flight attendant shut the door to Denali Air flight #4338 at 4:03 p.m. Five minutes later, the two-engine prop rose slowly into the blue afternoon sky, the morning fog now just a bad memory. We banked sharply to the left, crossing over the shimmering waters of the Cook Inlet, then passing above a marshy area traversed by winding ribbons of small rivers looking like something in an abstract painting. Reddish fingers of silt and silver ribbons of foaming white water striped the receding land below. At 16,000 feet, I could trace the rivers back to their origins at the sheer ends of mountain-hugging glaciers, the snow-dotted black peaks in the distance appearing as a storm-tossed sea of granite spanning to the horizon, waves of solid stone forever frozen in time.

With my nose pressed against the window, I marveled at the fierce beauty of a mountainside torrent cascading in sparkling fans of spray and foam from a high glacier down a nearly vertical rocky gorge. I was only vaguely aware of the conversation around me—talk of silvers and rainbows, the merits of three-by versus four-by leaders. I half-listened to the banter, Larry jostling me in his excitement as he discussed the fine points of fly tying with Babcock, his booming voice filling the cramped airplane. In the past, I would have been embarrassed at his need to be the center of attention. Now, I couldn't help but appreciate his happiness and excitement as the stunning views below brought home the reality that he'd made his life-enabling dream of traveling to fish in Alaska come true. I sat back in my seat while Larry and the others debated, argued, and laughed, conscious of my own satisfied smile, happy for Larry's happiness.

And then a shout from the front of the plane. "Shut the fuck up back there! We're trying to get some goddamned sleep!"

For a moment, it was as if someone had clicked off a radio that had been tuned to a fisherman's talk show, the good-humored banter replaced by a tense quiet, filled by the drone of the props spinning outside.

The quiet didn't last long. "Eat me, asshole!" Larry shouted.

"Eat yourself, dipshit!" came the response from the front of the plane.

"Eat your mother!"

"Too late. I just finished yours!" And with that, an arm poked up high over one of the seats, the raised middle finger of the hand pointing to the roof of the cabin.

Larry unclicked his seat belt and made a move to stand. I grabbed his wrist, stopping him just as he lifted off his seat. He dropped back down and glared at me. "What the hell do you think you're doing?" I whispered.

"That's my business."

"Forget about them. We land in Nalunaq, they go their way, we go ours, and we never see them again." He stared at me and wrenched his wrist from my grip.

"Fuck your wimpy philosophical bullshit. It's not the way I live my life."

"Live the life you want, but don't start a fight on a plane, for Christ's sake. Please. *Please*?" Larry shot me a look of disgust and slumped back into his seat.

I turned away and stared out the window, trying to calm my shaking. Far below, the land flattened, covered by an endless forest. No roads marred the vast carpet of trees and the shimmering ribbon of river directly beneath us. On the map I had brought with me, I could see that we were following the Kuskokwim River almost due west, into a sun still high overhead at just after 6 p.m.

We began our descent, I swallowed to clear my ears. I tried to spot the town and landing strip; unless our plane had sprouted pontoons, there didn't seem to be anywhere to land except for the river. And then I saw it—a tiny finger of land bounded by the Kuskokwim to the north and a tributary of the Kuskokwim—the Nalunaq River, according to the map— flowing to the east. Clusters of roofs huddled around a dirt runway looking like a tiny scratch in the surrounding forest, the village appearing as a mere foothold of human existence within a vast and still-dominant wilderness. We overflew the runway, banked, and dropped quickly, hitting the ground hard just moments after the plane had straightened.

Autumn-cool air flooded in through the opened cabin door smelling of pine and wood-fire smoke; a welcome change from the suffocating August heat and soggy humidity I'd left behind just the day before in Bethesda. I took a deep breath. The effect was magical, as if my anxieties and doubts surrounding the trip, the tension between me and Larry that had flared inside the plane, disappeared into the cool, sweet-smelling Alaskan air.

The magic didn't last long.

The hunters exited first, their boots landing heavy on the metal steps extending from the doorway. I was relieved to see them march off across the dusty runway to the squat, clapboard structure that served as the terminal building before Larry and the rest of us squeezed ourselves out of the plane.

Our group gathered in a tight circle just beyond the wing tip as I made my way down the stairs. Larry, exiting right behind me, pushed past and hurried to join them. As I came closer, I recognized Wiley Williams standing in the center, looking just like the picture on the brochure Larry had sent to me. His faded khaki, short-sleeved shirt fluttered on his wiry frame like an old battle flag. He wore a floppy, wide-brimmed hat and a pair of cargo pants, both the same drab color as his shirt, the hat casting a shadow over his face down to his stringy red beard. Babcock gave Wiley's hand a vigorous shake. "How the hell are you?" Babcock said.

"Doin' just fine," Wiley said.

Two young men stood alongside Wiley. The smaller of the two sported an unkempt beard that matched Wiley's except for its auburn color. "This here is Butch, my older boy," Wiley said as he set his hand on his son's shoulder. He then placed a hand on the shoulder of the other young man. He had white-blonde hair and a broad smile within a bushy, golden beard, his shoulder muscles and biceps bulging outside his sleeveless T-shirt. "This is Zack, son number two. When they say somethin', you listen. Got it?"

I noticed two women standing behind the young men. The first wore faded blue jeans and a rust-colored polo shirt, her close-cropped dark hair covered by a New York Yankees baseball cap. The other, taller woman sported a black tank top and khaki shorts, stylish leather sandals on her feet. She swept her finger across her forehead, clearing a few stray strands of wind-tossed, wispy red hair from her eyes. Girlfriends of the sons, I guessed, although they both seemed older than the muscular twenty-somethings assisting their father.

"Go on and collect your gear," Wiley said. "Truck's waitin' outside the fence. Butch and Zack can help get your stuff loaded."

A bullet-scarred front-loader parked on the far side of the runway belched out a cloud of exhaust and creaked its way on steel treads toward the plane. The driver maneuvered the bucket close to the opened hatch on the underbelly of the fuselage. Two men climbed inside the plane and tugged the hunters' coolers to the lip of the hatch, cursing as they strained to lower them into the bucket.

I headed for the terminal as the luggage men climbed back inside the fuselage. Wiley and Zack stood outside the door. "You're Larry's brother," Wiley said.

"Yeah, that's right."

"You decided to come after all. Your brother wasn't sure you would."

I forced a smile. "Neither was I, but here I am," I said.

"Well, that's good, I guess." Wiley seemed to shrug before heading toward his flatbed sitting outside the chain link fence circling the airfield. I was about to step inside when Zack's heavy hand grasped my shoulder. He glanced back at his father and leaned closer to me. "Don't you worry none about my dad," Zack whispered. "He gets kinda ornery when a trip's beginning. He's all right, you'll see," he said and smiled. "What's your name?"

"David Nichols."

"Nice meetin' you. I'm Zack. You ain't a fisherman, are you?"

"Not really."

"I figured."

"How?"

"Dunno, just can tell sometimes. So, you ain't?"

"A fisherman?" I said. "Nope. Not even close."

"Good. I like it when someone's on the trip who ain't a fisherman. Means I got someone to talk to. Mind if I ask you a question?"

"Ask away."

"If you ain't a fisherman, why'd you come?"

"My brother invited me."

"One of them bonding experiences?"

"I guess."

"Well, good luck with that."

We stood there for a moment. His reluctance to step inside and join the others seemed almost as strong as my own. "So how about you? Doesn't sound like you're all that into fishing."

"I just work with my dad and my brother," he said. "It's a living, for now. Not gonna spend my life doin' it, though. No way." He glanced at me sideways, seeming to size up my trustworthiness, then shot a look back toward the truck. Wiley's back was toward us, his elbows resting on the hood, his eyes fixed somewhere high above the broad levee protecting the village from the Kuskokwim. "You ain't never going to catch me with a rod in my hand," he whispered.

"Why's that?"

He shrugged. "Don't know. I mean, I think it's cool to watch the guys who really know how to do it, the line all played out, arching through the air against a sun freshly risen, steam still on the water, those little drops on the line glistening like diamonds—I get all that. It's just not me."

My surprise at Zack's aversion to fishing was nothing compared to my amazement at his lyrical description of the activity. "So, if you don't mind me asking, what are you thinking about doing?" I said.

"If I knew, I'd be doin' it." He looked down at the ground, the tip of one of his beat-up hiking boots toeing the dust, then sighed deeply as if reinflating himself. "We better get our asses in there with the others. If my dad turns around and sees us, he'll be mighty pissed."

"Quick question," I said. "The women, they're friends of yours?"

"Them? Shit no. They're on the trip, just like you and everybody else. The one with the Yankees cap is from New York—like duh, right? But that's about all I know. We get women comin' with us every so often, maybe once every other season. Not that big a deal for us; just means we bring along an extra potty shovel." Zack smiled and clapped me on the shoulder. "Good talkin' to you, now I gotta get to work."

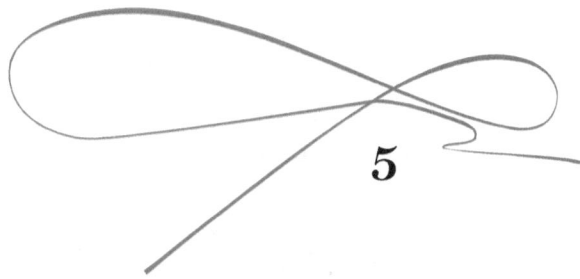

5

I stepped inside the shack to the rusty squeals of the garage-style metal door grinding open. A rush of diesel-fumed air from the front loader idling outside filled the room, its half-raised bucket crammed with luggage. The two luggage men hopped down from their riding place on the serrated edge of the bucket, lifted the bags and tossed them through the opening onto a dented metal slide. The bags skidded down and crashed to a stop against a battered wooden rail.

My bag was one of the first hurled in. I retrieved it and carried it back to the exit door and out of harm's way. The next bags crashing down the slide belonged to Babcock, Carl Cooper and Bob Billings. The military-issue duffel that followed belonged to the dour-faced guy whose name, I learned, was Rick Garrett. Garrett took hold of the duffel and walked past me, his vacant blue eyes not giving me a look as he headed out the door.

The hunters' bags came next. Each moved his bag off to the side before they regrouped around the slide as the luggage men climbed back into the bucket of the front-loader. The driver throttled up the engine, blasting another thick cloud of diesel fumes into the terminal. The machine shuddered.

Its bucket swiveled downward, the men crouching inside coming into view alongside the coolers.

The men slid each of the coolers forward, the plastic bottoms scraping against the grit on the bucket floor. They positioned the coolers on the teeth of the bucket's edge, hopped down and wrapped their arms around the sides of the first cooler. They swung it forward and crashed it down on the slide, the second one following.

The hunters lifted the coolers onto the floor and opened the tops, inspecting their cargo for any damage. "Looks good," T.J. said. "Close 'em up and let's get 'em on the truck." A couple of the hunters grabbed the handles and rolled them out the door.

With the hunters gone, the room fell silent but for the throbbing of the front-loader's engine. Larry and the others pressed close to the end of the bag slide, watching in stunned confusion as one of the unloaders flipped a switch on the side of the outside wall, starting the door on its creaking descent.

"What the fuck, man?" Larry cried out from the dim, diesel-smelling darkness of the room. "Where the fuck is my bag?"

"Where the fuck are *our* bags?" Russ wheezed. "You ain't the only one who's missing your shit."

A quick glance confirmed that the luggage for Paul Acer, Tommy Ewing and Tony Giordano also hadn't arrived. "Holy shit," Zack said. "The fuckers did it again."

"Did what again?" Larry said. *"Did what again?"*

"Don't you worry none," Butch said. "We'll take care of it."

"You goddamn better take care of it," Larry shouted as Butch and Zack rushed out the door. "My flies are in my bag and my bag ain't here!" he cried out. *"All my fucking flies!"*

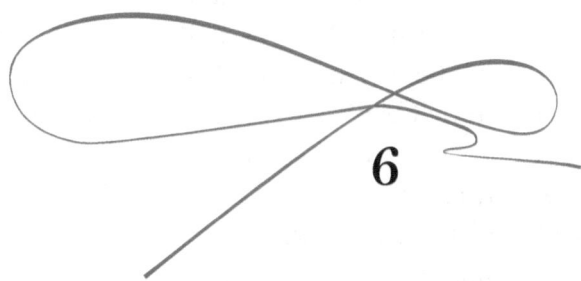

6

Butch and Zack headed for the truck. Wiley sat on the open tailgate, his legs dangling off the end. "Goddamn if fucking T.J. didn't do it again," Butch shouted.

"Do what?" Wiley said.

"That bag shit."

Wiley's head dropped forward, looking as if he'd been shot. "What happened?" he said.

"We only got luggage for five of our guys. Meanwhile the fucking hunters got all their shit, including their goddamn coolers that weigh about a ton each."

Wiley shook his head, his scrubby beard brushing his shirt. "First off, I'd like you to stop your cussin'," he said without looking up. "I didn't raise you in the street and don't go thinking you can talk like that around me just 'cause your mother ain't around no more to hear it."

"Yes sir," Butch said.

"Now, you're sure about the bags?"

"Unless they still got 'em back in the plane."

"Well, then, sounds like we gotta check out the plane before we jump to any conclusions."

Wiley hopped down from the truck and hustled past me,

his sons half a step behind. Larry and the others emerged from the building just as Wiley and his sons passed by. "My fucking bag's not here," Larry said. They didn't stop. "All my fishing gear's in that bag!" Larry shouted. "Every one of my goddamned flies—*every one of them*!"

Wiley, Butch, and Zack pressed on toward the plane, Larry and the others hustling to catch up. The white-haired pilot sat on the extended stairs, smoking a cigarette despite the NO SMOKING sign we'd just walked past. His co-pilot leaned up against the fuselage in the shadow of the wing, watching us. "Keep 'em here," Wiley said. Zack and Butch stopped, arms out like overgrown school crossing guards.

"Some of my people didn't get their bags," Wiley said.

The pilot sucked in a long drag and blew the smoke out a corner of his mouth. "That's all we got, far as I know," he said.

"You sure?"

The pilot turned toward his co-pilot in that slow, painful way that people do when arthritis has settled into their neck. "Hey Pete, we got any bags left?"

"Nope."

"Mind if I take a look?" Wiley said.

"Knock yourself out," the pilot said.

Wiley pressed himself up and into the fuselage. For a moment I allowed myself a glimmer of hope, a belief that Wiley would find the bags in the deepest recess of the hold. A few moments later, Wiley appeared empty handed. He jumped down and brushed off his pants. "Where are they?"

"Back at Anchorage, I guess," the pilot said. "Look, I just fly these planes, I don't load them. How the hell should I know?"

"You should know because it's your goddamned plane!" Larry shouted over Zack's shoulder.

Zack turned toward Larry. "It would be really smart if you'd just shut the fuck up right now, okay?" he said.

"So, when are you bringing those bags?" Wiley said.

The pilot knocked a column of ash from his cigarette. "This is the last flight today. Seeing that this place is closed to us on Sunday, I'd say you can get those bags in here by Monday noon if there's room on the morning plane. If not, you're talking about Monday afternoon. Tuesday at the latest."

"Ain't gonna cut it," Wiley said. "I got a Cessna comin' in here tomorrow to take us up into the back country. We gotta keep to the schedule or we won't make it back down the river in time to get these folks out of here. The pilot ain't available any other day anyways."

"Looks like you got yourself a problem," the pilot said.

"Those coolers weigh more than all my people's gear put together. How much you get for that?"

The pilot narrowed his eyes. "How much I get?"

"Yeah. How much of the cut was yours?"

The pilot dropped his cigarette and ground it out beneath his heel. He stood up and shaded his eyes from the sun still high in the northwestern sky. "I ain't even going to bother to answer that," he said. "What you say we get on back, Pete? I don't need this bullshit."

"The last time one of your pilots pulled this, he got in a heck of a lot of trouble," Wiley said.

Pete shut the door to the luggage compartment, climbed the stairs, stepped inside the plane. The pilot followed, stopping on the platform just outside. "Trouble?" he said. "Trouble, my ass." The steps retracted, the cabin door slammed shut. The engines cut on, the wind from the propellers lifting the hat off Wiley's head. He snatched it before it hit the ground.

The plane throttled up, sped down the runway, lifted off. I looked around for Larry and caught sight of him just as he raced past the terminal building, sprinting toward the hunters and their truck. Zack and Butch took off after him, looking like a couple of linebackers running the 40-yard dash in the football combines. By the time I caught up, the three of them were on the ground, Zack holding tight to Larry's ankles, Butch's knee in Larry's back, his hand pressing the side of my brother's face into the dirt. "Jesus Christ, let him up!" I shouted. Larry struggled to escape but Butch pushed down harder.

Wiley got down on one knee, staring into Larry's half-flattened face. "I'll tell my boys to let you up, but under one condition," he said. "You leave those guys to me. This is my trip. I'm responsible for everyone that's on it and everything that happens, got it? Pull one more stunt like that and your ass is on the first flight home."

Wiley stood up and nodded to his sons. They backed off. Larry got to his feet, wiping away grit stuck to his cheek. "Everyone stays put, and I mean everyone," Wiley said. He slapped the dust off his knee and headed toward the hunters.

Wiley said something to T.J., toeing the ground as T.J responded with words I couldn't make out. Zack tapped me on my shoulder. "T.J.'s a real fucker," he whispered. "Seems like every year he pulls some kind of bad shit. My dad's reported him a couple of times. Somebody from the state once threatened to pull his guide license, but it never happened. Fact is, nobody gives a shit about who does what to anybody out here."

"The airport's really closed on Sundays?" I asked.

"To commercial flights. Private planes can come and go."

"Any chance we can hire a pilot to fly the bags out here?"

"By tomorrow morning? From Anchorage? No way."

"What happened when T.J. did this before?" I asked.

"There's a little store close to the hotel. We got our people outfitted as best we could there. They don't have a ton of stuff, but they've got waders, boots, jackets, some cheap rods. Enough to get by."

"Flies?"

"Some made-in-China shit. Not great, but it all mostly worked out in the end."

I thought of Larry on the precipice of death, meticulously tying each of his flies in his dismal hospital room, his focus upon each bead and feather, each thread and knot, carrying him away from the pain and danger and fear to the beauty and promise of the Alaskan wilderness. Imagining all those magnificent flies trapped inside his duffel on the floor of a dark storeroom in the Anchorage airport infuriated me.

I took a deep breath and tried to clear my head. My bag was mostly filled with gear he'd given me. Even his old rod was in there. He could have all of it; he didn't need to go to some stupid little store to get outfitted with some cheap shit. I didn't even need to go on this trip. His flies weren't replaceable, but he'd have to deal with it. It would all work out in the end, just like Zack said.

T.J. turned away from Wiley and shut the tailgate of his truck. He climbed into the cab, started the engine, and rumbled down the dirt road toward the village, disappearing behind a cloud of dust. Wiley headed back our way. "Everyone in the truck," he said.

"What about the bags?" Russ asked.

"We'll talk about that later. We got dinner waiting for us back at the hotel. Billy don't like it none when we're late, so let's move."

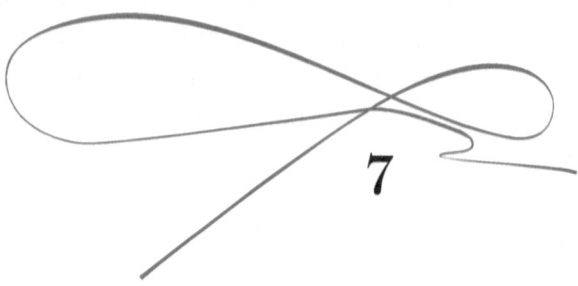

7

We bumped down the dusty road toward the Nalunaq Inn, the mood in the back of the rusty Ford pickup making me feel like I'd hitched a ride in an open-air hearse. Larry sat with his back against one of the sidewalls, head down, knees drawn up tight and clasped between his arms. I swung my legs around, letting them dangle off the edge of the open tail-gate as we drove through the village. We passed the haphazard scattering of wooden shacks on the narrow strip of land nestled between the levees holding back the Kuskokwim and Nalunaq rivers. Shirts and overalls, bras and underwear hung on rope lines attached to rough-cut poles in the front yards of the shacks. Strips of moose meat draped wooden racks, drying in the sun. Junked cars and an occasional demolished airplane lay scattered alongside cannibalized engines, the rusting remains littering the weedy ground like bones from long-dead carcasses.

Just before reaching the bend in the road at the point of confluence between the Nalunaq and the Kuskokwim, we passed a sign, black letters hand-painted on bare wood: **NALUNAQ DELTA STATE FAIR AUGUST 18 - 20: FIRE-WORKS FRIDAY!** I considered the dates and realized that we were due back here next Friday afternoon, just in time to catch the fireworks before our departure the following morning—if this trip actually happened at all.

The truck jerked to a stop and Butch jumped to his feet. "Nalunaq Hilton," he shouted. "Get your keys, wash up, and get ready for dinner. Leave your bags, we'll deal with them."

"I don't have my fucking bag," Larry growled.

Butch ignored him and waved at the red-haired woman. She smiled, nodded. He stepped up on the truck's sidewall, arms outstretched like an Olympic diver. He launched himself over the side, grabbing hold of his knees in a tight tuck and pulling off a full flip before sticking a perfect landing in the dust. "Goddamn hot dog," Zack murmured. "He's going to get in that chick's pants before this trip's over, you watch."

Wiley shooed us up the dirt path toward the front door of the inn. I followed behind the others, leaving Larry outside in his near-paralytic gloom. I stepped inside and waited as Billy, the white-haired, crooked-toothed, six-foot-seven-ish proprietor puffed on a cigarette and handed out the keys, giving everyone the same little speech in his smoke-coarsened voice, his instructions punctuated by smokey jets blasted out flared nostrils; "Rooms are in the out-building, down the hill to the left. Dinner's in exactly ten minutes. Don't be late." I noticed six picnic tables arranged in the hotel lobby to my right, each draped with a red-and-white checkered tablecloth. Not exactly haute cuisine but, under the circumstances it would do.

I approached the registration desk, the dark wood scarred by knife-gouged initials of people and places, dates as far back as July 1964. Billy delivered his speech to me and handed me a key. I figured I'd let Larry get his own key when he felt up to it. We were sharing a room in any case so at least we could get in and get ready in time for dinner.

I headed outside and coaxed Larry down the path to the out-building. We entered a narrow hallway lit by a single, wire-dangling bulb, and opened the door to Room 6. Larry flopped onto the bed along the far wall. I turned to close the door when the women entered the hallway. The redhead, her sunglasses perched above her forehead, smiled and walked past. Her friend paused and leaned close to me. "Is he going to be all right?" she whispered.

"I hope so," I said. She looked worried, seeming as if she wanted to say something more but only offered a tight smile before following her friend down the hallway.

I stepped inside our room and closed the door. Larry lay facing the naked sheetrock wall on the far side of his bed, his pillow wrapped around his head. For a moment, I wasn't sure if he was still breathing. "This is totally fucked," he mumbled into the pillow. "Totally, completely, one hundred percent fucked."

"It is a bit of a mess," I said.

"A bit of a mess? *A bit of a mess*!" Larry threw the pillow blindly in my direction. I caught it and clutched it to my chest. "This trip's over," he said. "Done. Finished."

"It's not finished," I said. "You're going fishing."

"Yeah? How's that gonna happen with my fucking bag still in Anchorage?"

I didn't have time to talk to him about his taking the equipment he'd given me. Billy's ten-minute warning was almost up, and he didn't look like the kind of person you wanted to piss off. "Let's discuss it after dinner," I said.

"I'm not going to dinner."

"Come on," I said. "You'll feel better after you get some food into you."

"I told you, I'm not going."

I checked my watch—only two minutes left. "I'll bring you back something."

I walked out into the low, golden sunlight of the mid-summer Alaskan evening and noticed the hunters' truck parked on a patch of weeds alongside the inn. *Maybe it was best that Larry decided to skip dinner after all*, I thought.

The hunters sat at the table closest to the inn's front door, their loud voices and boisterous laughter filling the room. Our group sat at three tables on the far side of the room. I looked for a place to sit. There was no place left at Wiley and Babcock's table. Another group sat at a second table, Rick Garrett perched on the end of one of the benches, separate from the others.

Zack and Butch sat at the third table along with the two women. The dark-haired woman who had been wearing the Yankees cap, the one who had stopped in the dingy corridor to ask about Larry, glanced over her shoulder. She smiled when she saw me and patted her hand on the empty space alongside her. Zack also saw me. He grinned and waved me over.

"Hey dude, where's your brother?" Zack said as I sat down.

"Still in the room."

The dark-haired woman leaned toward me. "How's he doing?" she whispered.

"Not great," I said.

"Don't think we've officially met," the redhead said. She leaned over the table. "I'm Angie," she said. I caught the scent of her perfume—heavily floral, perhaps gardenia?—as she extended her hand. Her fingers were long and thin, her hand as soft as any I could remember.

"David."

"David. Nice name." She smiled again and sat back down. "This is my best friend, Kathy," Angie said.

"Nice meeting you officially," I said. "And thanks for asking about my brother," I added softly.

"I think you better keep an eye on him," she said.

"Psychologist," Angie said. "Always worrying. That's why Kathy wanted to come way the hell out here, you know. Escape the city, get out into the wilderness, try to leave all those worries behind."

"What city are you escaping from?" I said to Kathy.

"New York."

"What part?"

"East Side."

"Upper or lower?"

"The Twenties," she said.

"Private practice?"

"Partly. I do some work out of one of the hospitals."

"Beth Israel or Bellevue?" I said.

She turned fully toward me. "Beth Israel. But how do you—you don't sound like a New Yorker."

"Neither do you."

She smiled. "Fair enough. What's your connection?"

"I trained at Bellevue."

Zack slapped his hand on the table. "Bellevue! I saw it in a movie once. Ain't that where they stick all the crazies?"

"Me among them," I said. He lowered his blonde brows, looking confused. "Don't worry, I just worked there. And it's a big hospital, not everybody's a psycho."

"You're a doctor!" Angie said.

"Kind of, I guess," I said.

"Well either you are or you ain't," Butch said.

"I do research. Haven't seen a patient in more than fifteen years."

An explosion of laughter from the hunters' table interrupted our conversation. "Hey, assholes, keep it down," Zack shouted.

"Fuck off," someone at their table shouted.

Things might have degenerated if Billy hadn't emerged from his kitchen balancing a giant round tray loaded with plates covered with metal warmers. A big bowl of salad rested in the middle. He put the tray down on an empty table between our group and the hunters and handed the salad bowl to Wiley. "Take what you want and pass it," he said. "Just make sure to leave enough for everyone 'cause I ain't got no more." Billy circled the table, uncovering the plates and setting them down in front of us: grilled halibut steaks, oven-roasted Yukon gold potatoes and asparagus. This and his salad—fresh, tender baby lettuce, sweet onions, and cherry tomatoes like I've never tasted before—would have ranked among the best dinners I'd ever eaten but my thoughts of Larry, lying alone and miserable in our room, pretty much killed my ability to enjoy the meal.

After Billy had served everyone, I noticed that there was one plate left on his tray. He looked around, shrugged, and carried the plate into the kitchen. I took another bite of my halibut, left my seat and headed toward the kitchen door. I was stopped by Butch's muscular arm. "Where you think you're goin'?" he said.

"To talk to Billy. He's got Larry's dinner. I want to save it."

Butch stared up at me. "You want Billy to save that dinner? No chance. If your brother ain't feelin' good enough to eat with everybody else, he ain't going to eat—period. Ain't that right, Zack?"

"Afraid so," Zack said.

"Well, it's worth a try," I said.

Butch looked at Zack, who just shrugged. Butch withdrew his arm. "Whatever you do, don't set foot in his kitchen," Butch said. "Ain't no one gone into his kitchen in forty years and lived to tell about it. Shit, last one who stepped foot in his kitchen ended up in a stew."

"Wasn't half bad, neither," Zack said and smiled.

I headed back to the kitchen and peered in through the open doorway. The room seemed oppressive, claustrophobic; long, narrow, and dark, an ancient, iron stove with six big burners and an industrial-sized, stainless-steel double sink along the far wall. I glanced around and spied the covered dinner plate sitting on a butcher block counter alongside the stove.

Billy threw open the oven door. The room filled with the delicious aroma of caramelized sugar. Billy pulled four Pyrex casseroles from the oven with dishtowel-wrapped hands, thick blue syrup bubbling out from beneath a layer of oven-browned crumbs. He set them down on the stovetop grating.

I knocked on the wall after he'd closed the oven. He turned toward me, grimacing as he straightened. "Stay right there," he said. "Ain't nobody sets foot in here 'cept me."

I gestured toward the covered plate on the counter. "Is that an extra dinner?"

"Yeah, and it pisses me off. Wiley says he needs fifteen dinners for his crew, so I make fifteen dinners. Looks like he counted wrong 'cause there's one left over. T.J. says he needs five dinners, so I make him five dinners and guess what? They eat five dinners. That's hunters for you, they got their shit together. Fisherman—?"

"Wiley counted right. The dinner's for my brother."

"Your brother? So, where the hell is he?"

"In his room."

"Well, tell him to get his ass in here."

"He can't. He's—sick."

"Sick?"

"Yeah."

"Too sick to come to dinner?"

"That's right."

"But not too sick to eat it?"

"I'm not sure. He may eat it, he may not." And then, thinking quickly, "but that halibut tastes so goddamn good, I just hate for him to miss it."

Billy's look seemed to soften. "Glad you liked it," he said.

"Liked it? I *loved* it! So did everybody else."

"Good to know. But you seen my sign out there? Says 'no food or drink in the rooms.' Food attracts varmints, and varmints are a pain in the ass, not for you but for me, 'cause I'm the one who's got to hunt 'em down and kill 'em. So, what's wrong with your brother?"

"Don't know, exactly. May be all the travel's gotten to him."

"You come a long way? Stupid question, everywhere's a long way from here. So, where you from?"

"Just outside of D.C. Larry's from Philadelphia."

"That's a pretty goddamned long way. Well, since you 'preciated my cooking, I'll let you have the dinner, so long as you promise me he ain't going to get a crumb, and I mean not a fucking speck of a crumb, anywhere in that room. Promise?"

"He'll be careful. Swear to God and hope to die."

He held the covered plate out to me then yanked it back. "But I ain't sendin' him no dessert. That's a blueberry cobbler I got there in them casseroles, and even one little blueberry makes an awful mess. He wants dessert, he's gotta haul his sick little ass into the dining room. Got it?"

"Got it."

I sat back down alongside Kathy and put the covered plate on the table. "He gave you the *dinner*?" Butch said. "To take back to the *room*? Billy ain't never allowed no one to take nothin' back to a room. What the hell you do, tell him you're going to find him a wife or something?"

"Billy ain't got no use for a wife," Zack said. "He'd be better off with a new set of knives."

After everyone had finished, Billy emerged from the kitchen carrying his big tray and a dented steel bucket. He set them both down atop an empty table next to us, collected the plates, scraped the few leftover slops into the bucket and stacked the empty dishes on the tray. He grunted and hoisted the tray with both hands, headed back into the kitchen, and returned for the bucket. "You all sit still now," he said as he wiped sweat from his forehead with a greasy corner of his apron. "I got blueberry cobbler comin'."

"*I got blueberry cobbler comin'*," Butch mimicked in a singsong after Billy had gone back inside his kitchen. "Well, shit, ain't that news. Every time we're here, it's blueberry cobbler. You'd think he was announcing the Second Coming."

"I *love* blueberry cobbler!" Angie gushed. "It's my *absolute favorite*!"

"Well, if you love cobbler, you're going to just plain have an orgasm over this one—if you don't mind me saying so," Butch said.

Angie smiled. "I don't mind at all," she said. I felt Kathy twitch. Angie flinched and reached beneath the table to rub her leg. She scowled at Kathy and turned her attention to me. "So, you say you do research. What kind of research do you—research?"

At that moment, it wasn't something I wanted to talk about. "It's kind of boring," I said.

"I'll bet it's not," Angie said. "Come on, tell us."

"Well, okay, but don't say I didn't warn you. I study apoptosis."

My tablemates fell silent. I'd seen this effect before, it was a great way to end unwanted conversations at parties. "A-pop-*what*?" Zack finally said.

"Apoptosis. Programmed cell death. It's the way cells die. Some people don't pronounce that second 'p', but I do."

"Sounds like he was right," Butch said to Angie. "Pretty goddamned boring."

Billy returned with his cobblers, setting a bubbling, sweet-smelling casserole dish down on each table. "Dig in," he said.

It was the best dessert I ever tasted; at once sweet and tart and smooth and crunchy, the warm, soft, syrup-covered blueberries popping on my palate in explosions of exquisite flavor. I wanted to say something to Billy, but he'd retreated to his kitchen before I could say anything.

For a moment, I lost myself in the glorious gustatory experience; my tensions surrounding Larry and his lost fishing flies seeming to dissipate like a lifting psychic fog with each forkful of Billy's exquisite blueberry cobbler. And then Kathy put down her fork, stopped her chewing and sniffed the air. "Cigars!" she hissed.

Swirls of smoke, glowing in the sunlight streaming in through the front window, enveloped the hunters' table.

"They can't smoke cigars in here!" Kathy said.

"Why the hell not?" Butch said.

"Because it's disgusting!" Kathy said. "How can anyone taste anything if they're breathing in that horrid smoke?"

"Still tastes damn good to me," Zack said and smiled, a blueberry skin mostly covering one of his big upper incisors.

Kathy swung her legs over the bench and headed for the hunters' table, a napkin over her nose and mouth against the smoke. T.J. sat back in his chair and smiled. "Well, honey, what can we do for you?" he said.

"Smoking cigars inside is unhealthy and rude, especially in a restaurant," Kathy said. "Please take them outside or put them out."

"You see any no smoking signs?" a fat-faced hunter asked through a gap-toothed grin.

"Signs or no signs, you can't smoke in here. Now please put them out or leave."

"You orderin' *us* to leave?" The hunter's fat cheeks collapsed as he sucked in more smoke, releasing it in a gray-blue jet aimed at Kathy. "You don't like cigar smoke, sounds like it should be you who's leavin'."

T.J. looked toward the table where Wiley and Babcock sat. "Goddammit Wiley, we've been crossing paths up here for near seven years, and we ain't never had any problems to speak of—"

"'Cept when you assholes bribe the airline into carrying your booze out here and screwing us," Zack shouted out.

"Nothin' personal," T.J. said. "Anyways, what I was gettin' at was that things have been okay between us, and now you go and let these here women on your trip and it all gets fucked up—if you don't mind me sayin'."

The gap-toothed hunter pulled his cigar out of his mouth. "Shit, T.J., it makes all the sense in the world that there's women on a fishin' trip. No one better at handlin' rods than a woman."

Kathy snatched the cigar from his hand and ground it into what was left of his blueberry cobbler. "We're good with cigars, too," she said. "Especially dinky little ones like yours."

The hunter made a move to stand but Rick Garrett flashed across the room, grabbed the hunter's arm, and planted his face into the cobbler.

Benches scraped back and toppled. We were heading for a full-on brawl until Billy stepped out of the kitchen holding a meat cleaver. "Everybody freeze!" he shouted. "Swear to God, I'll castrate the next son of a bitch who moves. What the fuck's goin' on here?"

Garrett grasped a handful of his prisoner's hair and yanked his face out of the plate. "One of my party politely asked them to put out their cigars, but they just kept right on smoking," Wiley said, as devoid of emotion as a court stenographer reading a record of testimony back to a judge.

"Politely my ass," one of the hunters murmured.

"Goddamn it, T.J.," Billy said. "If I told you once I told you a thousand times, I don't really give a rat's ass if you want to smoke in here, but if someone else don't like it, you put 'em out. So do us all a favor and get your cigar-smoking asses out of here."

T.J. looked like he wanted to say something, then glanced at Billy's meat cleaver and apparently thought better of it.

He signaled for his troop to head outside. The gap-toothed hunter with streaks of blueberry cobbler still smeared on his face stopped at the door. "Have a good time," he said. "Nothin' like traveling light out there in the backwoods."

If anybody considered going after them, Billy and his meat cleaver put the thought out of mind. "I don't want no funny business with them outside, at least not here on my property," Billy said after the hunters were gone. "They'll go their way, you go yours, and let that be the end of it."

They'll go their way and we'll go ours, only our trip's fucked because of those assholes, I thought. *Totally, completely fucked.*

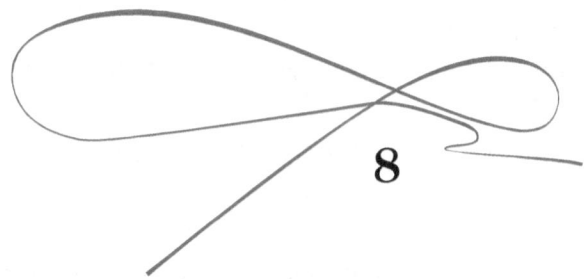

8

Billy returned to his kitchen, evidently convinced that his imposed peace would hold. I wanted to take the dinner back to Larry while it was still warm, but Wiley had other ideas. "Everybody follow me to the garage so you can repack your bags," he said.

"What if we ain't got no bag?" Russ called out.

"We'll deal with that," Wiley said. "I've got a fix in mind. It's not perfect, but it'll get you all out there."

I took Larry's dinner and followed Butch, Zack, and the rest down a gravel path around the far side of the hotel to an oversized, dimly lit garage smelling of oil and damp concrete. They had the bags laid out in a semicircle, each with a black, waterproof duffel draped across the top.

"Everything except your rods and reels needs to go into your water bag," Wiley commanded. "Whatever don't fit, stays; no exceptions." Angie stood alongside her canvas suitcase, embroidered with bouquets of pink and white lilies, looking panicked.

Wiley pulled a well-worn piece of paper from his back pocket and unfolded it. "This here's the packing list I sent you," he said. "If you followed it, you're good to go."

Angie raised her hand. "What if we brought just a teensy bit too much?" she asked.

"Then that teensy bit stays right here," Wiley said.

"Will it be safe?"

"From people? Sure," Butch said. "It's the bears you got to worry about. They'll smell all that perfume in that flowery bag of yours and they'll rip the shit out of it."

Zack smacked Butch an open-handed blow on his back. Butch burst out laughing. "Just playing with you. Ain't no bears, least not around here." Angie exhaled, her hand over her heart. "'Course the snakes'll find it a nice place to nest," Butch whispered to Zack.

Wiley shot Butch an annoyed look and glanced at his list. "Just as a reminder, here's what goes: Two pair of pants. Two long sleeve shirts, flannel or wool. Underwear for five nights. Rain suit with a hooded jacket, but no ponchos."

"But I brought my poncho," Carl Cooper whined. "Why no ponchos?"

"We're gonna be spendin' most of our time on a river," Wiley said. "Sometimes people fall off. You ever try to swim in a poncho? I can tell you haven't 'cause you're still alive. Now listen up for the rest: Polarized sunglasses and pocket-knife. Dacron sleeping bag, rated to 20 degrees or less, in a compression stuff sack. Head net, insect repellent, tobacco, and a small flask of spirits—but no beer."

"Those assholes brought beer, and I'll bet a whole lot else, and screwed us over," Russ murmured.

"We're going to fix it as best we can," Wiley said.

"How?"

Wiley sighed. "Everyone who has his gear, go ahead and put it in your stuff sack and you're good to go." He folded the list and jammed it into his pocket. "There's five of you who didn't get your bags, right?" He glanced at the bagless group and counted four with his finger, then turned to me. "You better be sure your brother gets this message. I ain't about to repeat it."

"Yes, sir, I will," I said.

"Good, so here's what we're going to do. There's a little store close by to our hotel. It's usually closed by now, but I stopped in and asked them to stay open so's you could gear up. It ain't the best store in the world, but it ain't the worst, either. They've got the basics, and they also have decent fishing tackle. I'm also asking that you guys who have your stuff share what you can, 'cause they jacked up the price of most of the stuff in there. You guys with no bags, follow me."

I held tight to Larry's dinner plate and followed Wiley toward the store. As we passed by the annex, I ducked inside. I entered my room quietly, hoping to find Larry asleep, hoping that the nap might make him feel a little better. He lay pretty much as I left him, flat out on his bed, the pillow he'd thrown at me once again wrapped around his head.

"Get the hell out," he said.

"I brought you some dinner."

He sat up, his face red. "I told you I didn't want any dinner."

"Wiley said there's a store with clothes and supplies. He's there now with the other guys whose bags didn't make it."

"Not interested."

"That's up to you." I set the dinner plate on the desk, pulled the chair out and swung it around. I sat facing him, my arms folded across the top of the backrest. "So here's what I'm thinking. Just about everything in my bag is yours. That means that you can use your own stuff. I'll go to the store and buy gear for me. Problem solved."

"Problem solved? What about my flies?"

"Larry, if I could do anything, *anything*, to get your flies back, I would, but I can't. Look, we're out here in Alaska, together. Alaska!" I got out of the chair and paraded around the room, imagining myself as a football coach trying to rally his team after a first-half thumping. "We're here with Tyler Babcock! It's going to be great fishing and a great adventure! Let's consider this a scouting trip; we'll have a good time now and then we'll come back, maybe even next year, and do it again, only this time with your flies! You'll have time to make more of them, maybe even better ones. Think of all the stuff you're going to learn from Babcock! And it's more than just fishing, Larry. How many times do we get to be together like this? And don't forget the lights!"

"The *lights*? What the fuck are you *talking* about?"

"The northern lights! You know, aurora borealis! Like on that big poster you had in your hospital room. All your life, you've said you wanted to see—"

"Fuck the lights. Fuck fishing. Fuck you. I'm not going without my flies."

"Look, we cleared our busy schedules and spent a ton of money to come on this trip. We're here, and we're going. I'm heading over to the store to get myself some gear. Zack and Butch are in the garage behind the hotel helping people pack their stuff into waterproof bags. Have some dinner and go get that done before they leave. I'll meet you over there with my new gear." He sat there, silent as a stone.

"Please have some dinner," I said. "It's really good, grilled halibut and potatoes. It'll make you feel better." I was halfway out the door when I had a last thought. "Just be sure to eat at the table and not in the bed," I said. "The manager's a pretty tough dude. He says that if you get a crumb anywhere, he'll kill both of us."

I forced a smile and closed the door. I heard the squeak of rusty springs. Good, I thought, he's going to feel so much better after he eats some dinner. And then—

SMASH! I heard the dinner plate shatter against the door, the tinkle of metal utensils hitting the floor.

Fuck!

I stifled my impulse to give Larry hell and hurried outside, figuring that the quicker that the mess got cleaned up, the better. I sprinted toward the garage and found Zack watching Kathy repacking her things while Butch helped Angie cram her lacy black undergarments into her stuff sack. "Grizzly been chasing you?" Zack said as I stood there, panting.

"I wish," I said. "You think you can get me a roll of paper towels?"

"You spill something?" And then— "Not the dinner."

Kathy looked up from her crouch alongside her bag but said nothing.

"I don't want to talk about it. Everything's under control."

Zack grinned. "Tell me you didn't spill the fucking dinner."

"I didn't spill the fucking dinner." Technically true.

"You better not have, or Billy'll cut your nuts off."

"Haven't had much use for them, anyway," I said. "Now can you please get me those towels?"

"You got this?" Zack said to Kathy.

"No problem," she said. Zack flashed me a thumb's up and jogged off toward the hotel. "You all right?" she said. "What happened?"

"Tell you later," I said, and headed off after Zack.

I followed him to the front door of the hotel and waited just outside. I could hear Zack and Billy arguing, but I couldn't make out what was being said. After a couple of minutes, Zack came out holding two rolls of paper towels. "Billy's a tough old bastard," he said. "But it's like with everybody, you just gotta know how to deal with him."

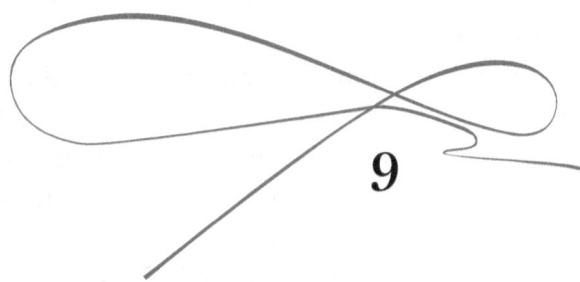

9

I was surprised to see Kathy standing outside the door to the bedroom annex. "Hey," I said. I tried hiding the towel rolls behind my back.

"The dinner spilled, didn't it?"

Actually, it was thrown. "No," I said.

"I was just in there, David. It smells very fishy."

I pressed the rolls of paper towels against the sides of my head as if to keep my brains from exploding. "Kathy, I am totally, supremely screwed," I said.

"Sounds like you could use some help."

"I can handle this."

"Speaking as a board-certified psychologist, I'm not so sure."

"Wait here, okay? I'll be out in a minute." Once inside the hallway, I could see—or smell—what she was talking about. I wasn't sure what would happen when I opened the door to our room. I jiggled the doorknob and listened—all quiet inside. I turned the knob, cracked the door open, waited, opened the door a bit wider. I eased my head through the opening. Larry wasn't there. I opened the door halfway, heard the broken plate scrape against the wooden flooring. In the glare of the lone light bulb, I noticed Larry's boot print in the middle of the mess.

I went out to Kathy and handed her a roll of the towels. She scrubbed at Larry's tracks in the hallway while I attacked the glop splattered on the inside of the bedroom door. We wet down handfuls of towels in the common bathroom at the far end of the hall, scraped up everything we could, and wiped down the floor planks in the hallway with towels saturated with Angie's gardenia-scented body wash (Kathy's idea).

Kathy gathered the wet wads of paper towels containing the splattered dinner and the shards of shattered plate. She held them at arm's distance, trying to avoid asphyxiating on the mixed vapors of halibut and gardenia. "I noticed a dumpster behind the hotel," she said. "I'll get rid of this there. You better bring the rest of this stuff back to Billy and then look for your brother. And please be careful."

The dining room was empty and the kitchen dark when I arrived with the warming top and utensils. I'd considered possible explanations for the absence of the plate, finally deciding to tell Billy that I tripped and dropped it while walking back to the hotel. I approached the threshold of the dark kitchen and called out Billy's name but received no answer. I set the cover and utensils down on a table, pulled my notepad and pen from my back pocket, and jotted down a note to him about my imagined mishap. I folded the note around a twenty-dollar bill, figuring that would more than cover the expense of the lost plate, stuck it beneath the cover, and headed out to find Larry.

I found him sitting up against a big spruce down near the levee. I might have walked right past if my attention hadn't been drawn by the crack of a thrown stone ricocheting off a nearby boulder.

I stepped into view. "You alright?" I said.

"Jim-dandy."

"That sucked, you know. What you did back there."

"I'll clean it up."

"Too late."

He dug his fingertips into the loamy soil, pulled out another stone and bounced it in his palm. "That's your problem. You're always trying to be my mother." He flung the stone at the boulder. It sailed high, landing with a muffled crash in the thicket of undergrowth just beyond.

"You got that wrong, you know. I was trying to keep us from getting castrated by the owner." The next rock flew my way, missing me by a few inches. "Anyway, we cleaned up the mess—"

"*We?*"

"Doesn't matter. You might just say thank you."

"Fat fucking chance."

And that did it. "You know what? I'm really sorry that you got sick. It tore my guts out when you got your diagnosis, when the chemo failed, when I knew you'd need a marrow transplant. Seeing you imprisoned in that room, tying those flies even when you were feeling like shit. And it's tearing my guts out to think about all those beautiful flies sitting somewhere back in Anchorage—"

Crack went another rock.

"But right now, you've got to make the best of it. That mess back there, that stinking mess that I had to clean up—"

"You got help."

"Goddamn it! I am fucking sick and tired of you feeling so goddamned sorry for yourself."

He was on his feet and on top of me before I had time to turn around. I barely got my hands up before he ploughed into me and took me down. If my fall hadn't been cushioned by years of fallen spruce needles, I probably would've dislocated my shoulder. "Sorry for myself? You think I'm feeling sorry for myself? This from mister perfect hot-shot college fucker who goes off to medical school and becomes a hot-shot research scientist studying who the fuck knows? And I get stuck with running the family business, and then I get fucking cancer? Sorry for myself? Fuck that!"

The way he threw his weight around seemed vaguely, horribly familiar and I suddenly realized that for the first time in more than thirty years, I was heading for a headlock. Just as he was about to clamp down, my instinct for self-preservation kicked in. I shifted a bit, sliding my head down so that his bicep pressed on my forehead. That's the key I'd learned so long ago: get my nose out of there, because that's where it really hurts, especially when I'm wearing glasses and the bridge gets squeezed and digs itself in—the mark can last for days. "You think it was fun watching you and Dad go off on fishing trips?"

"You got fucking seasick."

True. "What about all those times I got left behind when you went to play golf with him?"

"You had allergies."

Also true; the seeds of my interest in immunology. But still. "I outgrew them," I said.

"When you were thirty."

"You grew the business. You're in Short Hills now."

"Big shit. Commuting twice a week from Philly on the New Jersey Turnpike? The traffic sucks."

"But you wanted it!"

"Yeah, right. Importing leather from Argentina. A great way to spend your time here on earth, especially after it's been cut in half because of fucking cancer, probably from breathing in all those toxic fumes from the tanneries. I turn eighteen, I want to get the hell away, but instead I spend two years living at home and going to goddamned community college and then get a crappy business degree so I could take over for Dad someday. And now it's all mine. Fucking wonderful."

His dissatisfaction with his involvement in our father's leather import business was a sad revelation to me. He ratcheted up the pressure on my skull. I imagined my cranium imploding like a squeezed egg. "You make twice as much as I do, probably more." More pressure. "You've got Tina and two great kids who love you. I've got zilch."

"Your fault. You had plenty of women interested in you, but you couldn't get over Emily—"

"Her name was Emma."

"Emily, Emma, who gives a fuck? And how about Rachel Levine? She loved you to death. Dad used to tell me how much he hoped you'd get Emma out of your head and stick with Rachel, but that wasn't going to happen, was it? Shit, even Cindy Wappinger."

Cindy Wappinger? I couldn't believe he'd bring up Cindy Wappinger, the only girl I could think about from third grade until seventh, when she and her family inexplicably moved away just as I was entering puberty. Not that it would have mattered anyway; for all the years we went to school together, Cindy Wappinger never once seemed to look my way. And now, with my head pressed to near exploding between Larry's bicep and forearm, he decides to bring up

Cindy Wappinger? "Cindy Wappinger! She moved out right after I started junior high."

"Yeah, I remember. You think I've got Alzheimer's on top of my cancer? She went with her mom to Wilmington after her dad had an affair with the wife of a local cop. Stirred up some serious shit in our boring neighborhood."

"Her dad had an affair? Seriously?"

"Yeah, genius. And with a cop's wife, that stupid asshole. Beat the crap out of him; lucky he didn't get shot."

"Where'd you learn all that?"

"She told me."

"Cindy Wappinger *told you*? Like, when?"

"Long time ago already. Saw her at a bar."

"Bullshit."

"No bullshit. In Rehoboth. Summertime, ages ago, way before I met Tina. She was sitting right there, two seats down."

"How'd you even recognize her?"

"Couldn't miss her. Even more gorgeous than she was at fifteen."

"She was thirteen when she moved out."

"Close enough. There was something about her face and all that flaming red hair that made me think I knew her. And then one of her girlfriends called her Wappy. *Wappy*—do you believe that? Anyways, I looked past this guy sitting next to me and said '*Cindy Wappinger?*' She turned my way and that was that."

"Damn."

"Damn is right. She didn't recognize me at first, I think I still had that scrubby beard that Mom always hated, but then I told her who I was and that I was your brother and her eyes lit up. First thing she said was how she had a crush on you back in sixth grade."

"Bullshit."

"No bullshit, man. I gotta tell you, she looked great; blue eyes, killer body, and that amazing hair. Dynamite in bed, too. That was one crazy August night."

My Cindy Wappinger? Dynamite in bed? With my brother? Now I went berserk. I flailed at him, landing a few solid blows near his left kidney. He arched his back and dialed up the pressure around my head another notch. It wasn't long before my thrashing left me exhausted. I went limp as a corpse, hoping to bore him into releasing me. Instead, the calm offered another opportunity for Larry to launch into a further discussion of his grievances. "You think I wanted to be part of that goddamn business? Coming home from those warehouses stinking of leather? When I was a kid, I used to love leather, the cool, smooth feel of it. Remember Mom's long leather coat, the way it smelled in the car? I used to think Mom smelled like that. I loved that smell. And now, you know what? I hate it. *Hate it*! Every time I walk into a storeroom, I want to puke because of that smell. Mom's smell. Pretty fucked up, don't you think?"

"Definitely."

"But you never had to deal with that bullshit because Dad never wanted you in the business. You go to fucking Johns Hopkins, you become a hot-shot scientist while I'm spending my life stuck in stinking leather storerooms."

"Labs smell bad, too. The first time I tried tissue culture, I almost threw up in the incubator."

Larry's sharp twist of my head shot down my neck into my upper spine. "I was like a big fucking pulling guard, blasting holes in the defensive line of life so you could run through and get all the goddamn glory, all the fucking TV cameras on you while I'm left there, sitting in the mud. I was like a goddamn child sacrifice, charred like barbecued ribs on the hellfire of Dad's expectations, while you just mosey through life. I'm fucking Isaac, only this time the angels didn't come down and stop Abraham from lighting his fucking blowtorch and roasting me alive. And then I get fucking cancer, and they irradiate me and poison the shit out of me, and I tie all those flies, and now they're left behind because of a bunch of douche-bag alcoholic hunters. Fuck it. Just fuck it."

A woman's voice called my name—Kathy! Larry released me and jumped to his feet. "Where you going?" I said.

"To find Wiley. I'm leaving on the first flight."

"That's not until Monday."

"Fine. I'll wait for Monday."

"What am I supposed to do?"

"I don't give a shit."

Kathy called out again. "Over here," I shouted.

"Maybe stick around," Larry said as he trudged away. "You might get lucky."

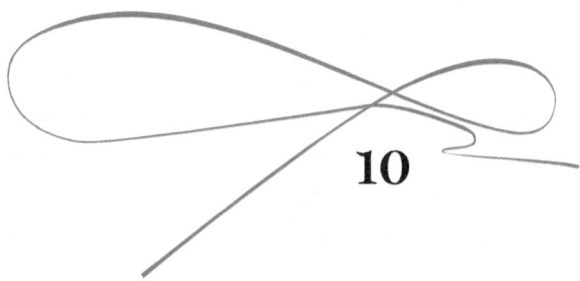

10

Kathy and I headed back to the dining room. She warned me that Wiley was getting agitated with both Larry and me for our absences during mandatory group meetings. He had just explained the schedule and logistics for tomorrow, she had volunteered to give us the information as well as share with us his displeasure. Wiley, meanwhile, had gone off to bed; a relief to hear as that meant that Larry couldn't deliver his decision to head home until the morning.

I wanted to detour from our route and climb the levee where the Kuskokwim and Nalunaq rivers converge, hoping that the view might help ease the ache in my head. The sun lay low in the sky, the twilight finally arriving at around 11 p.m. I always liked the way that rivers look and feel as the sun goes down—the deep greens and bug-ripples and the river smell—but Kathy worried about leaving Angie alone with a bunch of depressed and angry fishermen, especially since someone had talked about passing around a flask of whiskey after dinner. The last thing I wanted to do was to go back to that dining room but given all that she had done for me I had little choice but to go with her.

Inside the Nalunaq Inn the fishermen slouched on the benches, their stares empty, barely acknowledging our presence as we walked by. Kathy spotted Angie sitting with Butch and the Nashville group—Tommy Ewing, Paul Acer, and Carl Cooper. Kathy and I squeezed ourselves in at the table. "Feels like someone just died," Kathy said.

"I'll tell you what's died," Paul Acer said. "This fucking trip. That store sucked, they didn't have jack-shit. Now I got nothing to go with, so what the hell's the point?"

"The thing that pisses me off is that you and me, we live our lives for fishing," Carl Cooper said. "It's what we save our money for. It's what we take vacations for. It's what fucked up our marriages—mine, anyway. So, whose bags get left behind? Yours does, and his brother's," he said, looking hard at me. "Meanwhile he gets his bag just fine, and he don't give half a shit about fishing. Fucking sucks. SUCKS!" he shouted and slammed his fist on the table.

"It ain't his goddamn fault," Russ said from a neighboring table. "I bet he'd give anything so's that his bag was left behind and his brother's had come instead."

"Amen to that," I murmured.

"Mine's left behind, too," Russ continued. "But life's too goddamn short. I smoked my lungs near to death. The way things are going, in another year there's a damn good chance that I'm going to be hooked up to one of them oxygen tanks. Year from that, and I might be stone cold dead. So, you know what? I'm going on that trip tomorrow, bag or no bag. I don't give a shit if I have to wear the same goddamn pair of underwear for the next week."

"Glad I'm not sleeping in your tent," Paul Acer said.

"Yeah, well, my advice to all of you who got fucked over,

is get over it," Russ said. "Lewis and Clark made it halfway across the continent and back with less than what we got with us right now." I wasn't sure about the historical veracity of his statement, but I loved the sentiment. I just wished that Larry had been here to listen.

Russ's speech silenced the room. And then he said, "It's goddamned lucky that I don't need them heart attack pills stuck in my bag back in Anchorage."

I sat forward. "You've got pills in that bag?"

"Yeah, but no matter. I got that prescription about ten years ago, never had to use it. Still, my doc tells me to take the pills with me wherever I go. I'd just as soon forget about them, but my wife won't let me leave without them."

"You're not talking about nitroglycerin," I said.

"Sure am. Do you believe that shit? Before my doc gave that to me, I thought that was something you use to blow things up, not to keep people from having a heart attack!"

I got up from the table and walked over to where Zack and Butch were sitting. "How do I get in touch with the airline?" I said. "Like right now?"

"Use a phone, I guess," Butch said.

"Dumb shit," Zack said to his brother and turned toward me. "Billy keeps a number on a piece of scrap paper tacked up right by the phone in the kitchen. Dad got Billy to put it up there a few years ago when some guy from Florida got sick. Why do you want to talk with the airline? It's Saturday night?"

"I'll explain later. You think Billy would mind if I used the phone?"

"My guess is that he'd mind plenty," Butch said. "But you'll never know unless you ask him."

I had no choice. I'd turned off my cell phone since there wasn't any service out of Nalunaq. I approached the kitchen, hoping that Billy had gone to bed. It was dark inside, silent but for the whirring of the refrigerator at the far end. I smelled cigarette smoke and noticed an orange dot glowing near the far wall. Billy sat alone, the phone mounted on the wall just behind him.

"Billy, sorry to bother you." His cigarette flared. "It's me, David Nichols. We've got a problem."

"You're goddamned right you've got a problem. You busted up one of my good plates."

"I'm sorry. I paid for it."

"Yeah, well, you think I can just go and buy me a new one from some Walmart down the block?"

"Tell you what, I'll buy you a whole new set of plates. I'll send them to you air express."

Billy took another drag on his cigarette. "What'ya want?"

"I need to use the phone."

Billy coughed. "Why?"

"One of our guys is pretty sick, heart problems. His medicines are back in his bag in Anchorage. We've got to get them delivered by tomorrow or he could die. Right here in your hotel."

He dropped his cigarette and ground it out beneath his shoe. "Bullshit," he said. "He ain't needed none of them pills since the day his doctor gave 'em to him ten years ago."

He must have heard everything we'd been saying in the dining room. I decided to give him the straight story, explaining what Larry had gone through, how important this trip was to him, how it all meant nothing without those goddamned flies. I told him that, as far as Larry was concerned, his trip was over. Mine was, too, and from the way some of the folks out there were talking, there were more than a few who also were ready to give up. "I have a plan, all I need is the number for the airline. One phone call, that's it. Please."

Billy lit a fresh cigarette, shook the match out. "Okay," he said. "Make your call."

"Mind if I turn the lights on?"

"No lights. You turn them lights on now and I'll never get to sleep." He struck another match, lit the wick to a hurricane lamp, set the glass back on it. "This'll do," he said.

I held the lamp up to the collection of grease-darkened scraps of paper thumb-tacked to the drywall, found the number for Air Denali Medevac, punched it in.

"Yeah?" a voice said. I could make out sounds of a baseball game broadcast in the background.

"Is this the medevac line for Air Denali?"

"It's Air Denali. What'ya want?"

"Is this the medevac line?"

"Medevac line's closed."

"Since when does a medevac line close?"

"Since about eight. It's Saturday night, man."

"Look, I've got a medical emergency to report. Are you the right person?"

"Dude, I'm the only person you're gonna get at this hour. You wanna talk to somebody else? Wait 'till tomorrow."

"I can't wait until tomorrow."

"Then shoot."

I took a deep breath. "All right. My name is David Nichols. I'm a doctor with—with the National Institutes of Health in Bethesda, Maryland. I'm calling from Nalunaq with a medical emergency."

"What kind of emergency?" he said skeptically.

"There's a guy here, about sixty-three, with COPD and angina—"

"Look, buddy, I ain't no doctor. Is the guy sick or what?"

"Goddamn it, there's a fisherman out here who's about to have a fucking heart attack because your stupid-ass airline pulled his bag with all his medicines off the plane, along with the bags of four other guys on the trip. You know why they pulled those bags? Because some hunters bribed your guys to do it, so they could bring their booze coolers out here. This guy's going to keel over and die soon if he doesn't get his medicines. When he does, you and your goddamn airline are going to get your asses sued so bad, you're not going to have enough left to pay the electric bill. And did I mention jail time?"

"You need a medevac?" he said. "There's an army base not too far from there. I could get a chopper in there—"

Shit. "That won't be necessary. I think I can keep him alive overnight."

"You just said that the dude's about to die."

"He is—but there's someone else on the trip who takes the same medicines, and—and he has a couple of extra pills to spare. That'll keep him until the morning. Soon as the sun comes up, though, he's going downhill faster than a toboggan on a Denali glacier."

"So, what the hell do you want?"

"I want a plane in here no later than ten o'clock tomorrow morning. I want his bag in it, and the bags of the other four guys who had their stuff left behind on today's flight. You need names?"

"We only had two flights out to Nalunaq today."

"Actually, only one. The early flight got canceled. Fog."

"Good, makes it even easier. We got the names."

"Fine. So, are you going to do it?"

"You know that the Nalunaq airport is closed to commercial planes on Sunday, right? If you can't get it open, I can't do shit."

I had no idea how to open an airport. "Hold on." I set the phone down on the counter and went to see if Zack or Butch knew how to handle this. I stuck my head out of the kitchen door. "Zack, I got a problem," I said. "The guy from the airline says that he can't get a plane in tomorrow unless we can get the airport opened. Your dad says that they need to be on the ground by ten, or it'll be too late."

"Doc, you need the airport open at ten, it'll be open at ten," Zack said.

I picked up the phone again. "You're good to go tomorrow morning, no later than ten o'clock. And don't forget, we need all five of those bags."

"One? Five? Don't make no difference. You know what it's going to cost us to find a crew for a Sunday morning?"

"You know what it's going to cost you if this guy dies before you get here?"

He hung up before I could say anything else.

I don't remember much else about what happened after I announced that the lost bags would arrive the next morning. I do remember the look that Kathy gave me; not exactly a smile, more a look of bemused wonderment. I remember that look, but mostly I recall my sprint through the gloaming to tell Larry that his bag with his precious flies would be coming with us after all.

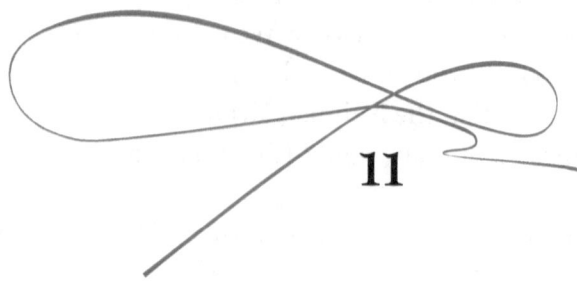

11

The impending arrival of the lost luggage dissipated Larry's gloom like warm sun on a morning fog. At breakfast, Larry snatched a seat alongside Babcock. They dove straight into a discussion on the strategy of fly selection; how the time of day, the weather, the speed of the current, even the extent to which the trees along the banks hung over the water—affecting light, water temperature, and the insects that the fish would be expecting to feed on—would be important to consider in making his choice of flies.

The absence of the hunters also contributed to the general good mood that morning. They had eaten earlier, marking their former presence with the stale odor of cigar smoke. We heard their chartered plane throttle up just as Billy was bringing out our breakfast, Russ flashing a raised middle finger toward the ceiling as the plane passed overhead.

I decided to skip the ride with the others in the back of the Ford and walk to the airport in the pleasantly warm morning, carrying the book I'd brought for the trip.

I'd barely started down the rutted road when I heard fast-moving footsteps behind me. I stopped and turned when I heard my name called, the sun lighting up Kathy's smile, her eyes shadowed by the brim of her Yankees cap. "Hey there," she said.

"Hi. No Angie?"

"She decided to ride."

"And you didn't?"

"Apparently not."

"Stupid question."

"I guess. I've heard worse."

"So, I'm not sure I thanked you," I said.

"For helping you clean up? It was the least I could do."

"Also for getting me out of a tight spot with Larry yesterday. It was lucky you called out my name when you did."

"I know. I thought he was going to squish your head if he didn't suffocate you first."

I felt the hot flush of embarrassment in my cheeks. "How much did you see?"

"Don't worry about it. I grew up with a brother, too." She glanced at my book. "What are you reading?"

"John McPhee. *Coming into the Country.*"

"Nice. I once took a class with him. You ever read *Basin and Range?*"

"With McPhee? Seriously?"

"Seriously."

"Where?"

"Princeton."

"You went to Princeton?"

"*Dei sub numine viget.*"

"Sorry?"

"The Princeton motto. 'Under the protection of God, she flourishes.' I bleed orange and black, along with half my family. What was your school's motto?"

"Hopkins? *Veritas vos liberabit.* The truth—"

"Shall set you free. I think I like it better than Princeton's. So, Doctor David—sorry, I've forgotten your last name."

"Not sure I told you. It's Nichols."

"Right, thanks. That was a strong performance last night on the phone."

"It got the job done, I guess."

"But, you know, doing what I do, I'm generally pretty good at getting a sense of someone pretty quickly. I've got to admit that you surprised me."

"Because I picked up a phone and transformed myself from a mild-mannered immunologist into a flaming, disingenuous ass? Be careful about first impressions."

"You weren't exactly a flaming ass. Disingenuous, maybe, but it was for a good cause. You saved the trip."

"Thanks, but let's see if the plane gets here when it's supposed to. I'll relax when I see Larry's bag. You weren't exactly what I expected last night, either. Small, cheap cigars? You almost started a riot."

"I guess that's what you get when you grow up with an older brother. Besides, I was pissed. Good thing Rambo was there to save my skin."

"Garrett's given me the creeps from the first time I saw him back in Anchorage. You know anything about him?"

"Nope. Angie and I arrived a day early and got to talking with Butch and Zack. Butch mentioned that he heard his dad talking about some ex-military guy, a Ranger or a SEAL or something, who was coming. That's got to be Garrett. Good that he was on our side last night."

"I guess."

"Be nice to him. I'm sure he'll be fine."

"I try to be nice to everybody."

"Of course you do." Kathy's laugh was lost in the sound of the truck approaching behind us. We scampered off to opposite sides of the road as it rattled past, leaving us in a cloud of dust.

We passed through the open gate in the fence around the airport and found the truck parked on a patch of weeds near the end of the runway. By the time we arrived, Butch and Zack already had laid out the waterproof duffels holding our gear. Three deflated slabs of heavy, rubberized canvas that would become our rafts lay in a stack near the row of duffels. Four industrial-sized plastic coolers stood alongside, each as large as the ones used by the hunters, next to a row of bear barrels packed full of dry goods for our meals.

The work slowed as 10 a.m. approached, our eyes stealing glances into the sapphire sky in search of the plane. Rick Garrett spotted it first, the withered skin around his hawk-like eyes creased in a tight squint against sun and distance. He signaled the approach of the plane with a raised right arm pointing at the speck of sun-gleaming silver descending between puffs of cloud. "There it is!" Tony Giordano shouted. If he said anything else, it was lost in the whooping and hollering that exploded from the group.

The plane overflew us, banked sharply, and landed in a puff of dust. The engines cut off, the cabin door opened as the short stairway extended from underneath. Out stepped the same pilot and co-pilot who had flown us yesterday, looking none too happy to be spending their Sunday morning back in Nalunaq. Pete, the co-pilot, walked past us as if we weren't there, straight to the baggage compartment door. He unlocked the hatch, yanked it open. The pilot knocked another cigarette out of his pack and lit it up. "You want 'em, go get 'em," he said.

"Get the bags, boys," Wiley said.

Zack pulled himself up and onto the floor of the baggage compartment and crawled inside. Two duffle bags appeared in the hatchway, then two more, and finally Larry's bag. Zack handed them down to Butch, jumped to the ground and dusted off the knees of his pants. He walked over to me, breathing hard, sweat on his brow. "That totally sucked," he whispered. "It's dark as a coffin in there."

"You boys done, 'cause we ain't coming back," the pilot said.

"Nothing else left inside?" Wiley said to Zack.

"Shit no," Zack said. And then he whispered to me, "except that big motherfucking bomb that just happened to drop out of my pocket."

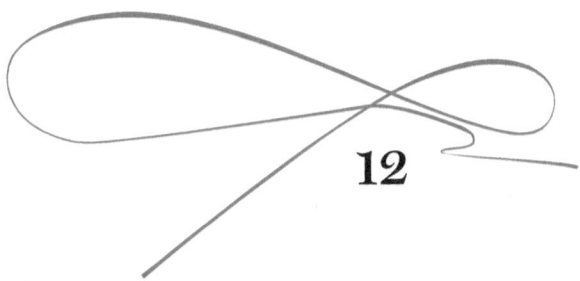

12

Wiley barked at Larry and the others who had just received their gear, hurrying them to repack into the waterproof bags he'd brought for them. "Luke's bringing our plane in any minute," he said, clapping his hands. "We've got four trips out to the headwaters. We gotta be ready to go."

I heard the engine's soft whine just before the plane came into view in the northern sky. It looked like it was going to overfly us and then bank leisurely to the west, allowing for a gentle landing at the far end of the runway and an easy taxi up to our truck. Just after the plane passed over the Kuskokwim, not a quarter mile from where we stood, the pilot rolled the plane up on its side, the wings perpendicular to the ground, turning and diving straight at us. The image flashed in my head of one of those horrible air race video clips, where a pilot rolls his plane too hard and flies it nose-first into the spectators, incinerating them in a ball of flames.

Before any of us could move, the pilot pivoted the plane around the tip of his lowered left wing, righting it just as he lined up parallel to the runway and sticking his wheels hard into the ground. I froze as he spun the plane one hundred and eighty degrees, kicking up a vortex of dust.

"Fucking Navy pilot," Rick Garrett muttered, the first words I'd heard from him since the beginning of the trip.

"What the hell was that about?" I asked Zack.

"Just old Luke, practicing," he replied.

"Practicing for what?"

Zack smiled at me in a funny kind of way. "You'll find out," he said.

The guy who climbed out of the pilot's door and walked toward us through the dissipating dust cloud had skin so pasty pale it seemed as if he had lived his life in a lightless cave, his bald head covered by a baseball-style cap bearing the *fleur-de-lis* insignia of the New Orleans Saints. "Hey Wiley," he called out. "Looks like we got us a great day for flyin'."

"Mornin' Luke," Wiley said, offering a two-fingered salute from the brim of his hat. "Nice landing. You still got tires left?"

The tires bolted to the landing struts beneath his orange and white Cessna 172 looked like nothing I'd ever seen before on a plane; fat, smooth, and treadless, reminding me of something you'd see on the back end of a dragster. "Shit, dat weren't nuttin'," he said to Wiley. "Just take a look at dem dere puppies." He gestured toward the tires with the pointed toe of one of his alligator boots. "Dey's brand new. Landed soft as a pilla."

Wiley gave him a look. "All right, let's load you up. We've got a lot of flying to do, and not much time to do it."

"Shit, Wiley, ain't more'n half an hour out, half an hour back."

"More like forty minutes, and then figure in loading and unloading, and then four trips. That's a good five hours right there. Then I gotta get things all set up out on the river and move us down to our first camp and get dinner goin' before everyone gets hungry and starts complainin.'"

"Glad I ain't in your shoes, buddy," the pilot said. "Too much stress for me."

Wiley whistled and signaled us to gather near him. He pulled a folded piece of paper from his pocket and shook it open. "Listen up," he said, his glance shifting between us and the creased sheet of paper. "We're going out in four groups. Group one: Richard Garrett, Anthony Giordano, Butch and me. We'll get the rafts down to the river. Group two: Tyler Babcock, Russell McPherson, Robert Billings, Thomas Ewing. Group three: Paul Acer, Carl Cooper, Kathy Sands, Angela Walker. Group four: Lawrence Nichols, David Nichols, Zack. You guys in the last group will be light on passengers, but there's probably going to be some bags left over, so that'll work out good." He clapped his hands rapid-fire. "Okay, let's get them rafts in first, and then as much of the gear as we can fit. Bags'll come later, and this time let's not leave none of them behind."

Butch and Zack crammed the four deflated rafts into the plane's hold, followed by the bear barrels and Wiley's duffel, then slammed the hatch shut. "Group one's ready to roll," Wiley said. "All aboard." Garrett climbed in first with Tony right behind. Butch was halfway in when he stopped and hopped back down. "Holy shit, almost forgot," he said, and jogged off toward the truck.

"Jesus, Butch," Wiley called out. "We ain't got time."

Butch emerged from the cabin of the truck holding up a shotgun and a dented-up cigar tin, the cartridges inside rattling as he jogged toward us. "Wouldn't want to forget these," he said.

"Damn," Wiley whispered. Butch flashed a smile as he passed by his father, slid the gun into the plane, then pulled himself up and into the cabin.

The plane lifted off and banked hard, following the Nalunaq River south into the wilderness. "What's the gun for?" I asked Zack when the plane was out of sight.

"Grizzlies, Doc," he said. He grinned and clapped me hard on my back. "Grizzlies."

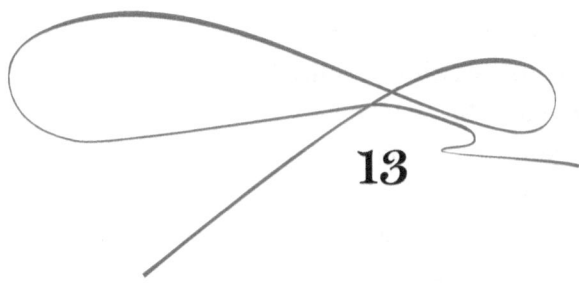

13

With Wiley and the plane gone, there was little else to do but kill time. Larry joined Babcock, Russ, Bob Billings, and the Nashville guys and headed toward a low stack of rough-hewn, pinewood shipping pallets piled on loose gravel off the other side of the runway. Zack drove the empty truck to the hotel, with plenty of time to walk back before the plane arrived for the second flight out. Kathy strolled with Angie down the runway, stopping at a patch of low weeds across the runway from the pallets. Angie knelt in the weeds and pulled off her pink cotton shirt, revealing a barely-there black bikini-bra on smooth, bronzed skin. She set her shirt on the weeds and laid down on it, her feet and face angled directly into the sun.

I stretched out atop a stack of sun-warmed pallets not far from where Larry and the others were standing with their fly rods, practicing their casting at a target Babcock had drawn with his boot in the dust. I read for a little while, John McPhee's book about Alaska serving both as an interesting diversion and shade against the sun. After I tired of holding the thick paperback up in front of my face, I put it down and pulled my hat over my eyes. I was almost asleep when I felt a kick against the sole of my right foot. Larry stood over me, silhouetted by the sun, holding his fly rod. "How about getting a little casting practice?" he said.

I yawned. "Maybe later?"

"Bro, you can't go out on that river without ever having casted before."

"You telling me that he's never used a fly rod before?" Babcock called out. He crossed the runway holding his fly rod. "Doc, lemme tell you something," he said. "You going out on that river without ever casting before is like me walking into an operating room saying that I can do brain surgery without ever having sliced open a brain. See what I'm sayin'?"

"Yeah, I guess," I said.

"We can't let that happen, right?"

"Apparently not," I said.

"Well then, get on up here and let's learn how to do it."

I took Larry's rod in my right hand, playing out some line in the fingers of my left just as Babcock was doing. Babcock talked me through it, emphasizing the need to keep the line tight at the tip, cautioning me about using too loose a wrist or too short a take-away or too long a follow-through. He demonstrated the technique, the rod becoming a perfect and natural extension of his arm, the motion drawn from a gentle yet firm back-and-forth of his right shoulder. He let the line play out with each cycle, curving off the tip of the rod in graceful arcs, growing longer with each motion until the release at the conclusion of the fourth cycle, right arm and rod fully extended in a statuesque pose, the small lead weight he'd tied near the end of the line drifting down and landing with a puff in the dust. "There," he said. "Now you try it."

I fiddled with Larry's rod in the fingers and palm of my right hand, trying to get a good feel before launching into my first cast. I glanced around and noticed the expectant eyes of the other fishermen, and from her seated position alongside Angie across the runway, Kathy.

I took a deep breath and twisted my shoulder backward to lift the rod as Babcock had shown me. I brought the rod forward, then backward, then forward again, glancing up over my shoulder, hoping to see a graceful arc of fishing line curving over my head. The line wrapped around the tip of the rod and dropped in a tangled mess at my feet.

The laughter of the fishermen was bad enough, but when I thought of Kathy witnessing this humiliation, I wished I could disappear. I glanced at her. She noticed and nodded, a signal not to worry, to try again.

"Knotting your line is a pain," Larry said as he straightened out the tangle. "You better practice all you can before we hit the river. This here is easy. Out there it'll be wet and windy, and you'll be doing this sitting down because we're going to be fishing from the rafts. It's going to be all upper body, and it's tricky. Isn't that right, Tyler?"

Tyler Babcock gave me one of those hopeless looks that you get when your coach is about to cut you from a team. "Afraid so, Doc. Practice right here might do you some good."

Larry seemed to have had second thoughts about giving his rod back to me, but then handed it over. "Just be careful with it," he said. "And if you feel like something's getting fucked up, stop and call me before it gets too bad to fix."

Just as I was about to give it another try I heard the whine of the plane engine. Luke LaDue brought the Cessna in easier this time. "Couldn't ask for a better day for flyin'," he said as he hopped down from the cabin. "Wiley don't like waitin'. Let's get her loaded up."

Zack, who had disappeared into a nap after returning from delivering the truck to the hotel, roused himself. We helped him pack more of the communal gear and as many duffels as we could fit into the hold of the plane. Tommy Ewing climbed in, followed by Bob Billings and Russ. Babcock squeezed his bulk into the seat up front, and LaDue closed him in. "Back in a jiff," he said. "Don't you go nowhere."

"*Don't you go nowhere,*" Zack mimicked as the plane disappeared in the southern sky. "Where the fuck am I supposed to go? Play me a round of golf? Pick up my sweetie-pie and go see a movie? Shit, I ain't got nowhere to go except back to sleep, so that's where I'm going. Do me a favor Doc, wake me when you see the plane." He headed over to a pile of pallets and ducked out of sight in their shadow.

I tried reading but I couldn't concentrate with the thought of my failure with the casting rod running through my head. Larry was right; it was insane that I didn't have the slightest idea of how to handle a fly-casting rod when I was about to spend nearly a week fishing in the wilderness. I set down my book and once again took up Larry's fly rod.

I practiced the motion a few times, keeping the line in at first, just trying to get a feel for the rod itself. I then played out some line with my left hand as Babcock had done, pulled back on the rod to get the cast started, played out more line with each subsequent motion, again and again and again and *released*—resulting in another tangled mess on the ground. Fortunately, Larry hadn't noticed, as he and the two remaining fishermen sat hunched over their fly boxes, studying the flies they'd tied.

I put the rod down and tried to untangle the line. A knot again had formed, too tight for me to undo with my clumsy fingers.

"Need some help with that?" Kathy approached, her smile sympathetic. "I'm pretty good at untangling messes."

"It's your job, right?"

"Cute. Here, let me see that." She squatted alongside me and untied the knot. "There, good as new. So now that that's done, how about I show you how this thing works?"

We walked aways down the runway, out of earshot of Larry and the others. I gave Kathy the rod, skeptical that she'd be able to show me anything I didn't know, which was basically nothing. She held it lightly in her fingers and began to swish it through the air. "The key is the rhythm," she said. "You've got to feel it, listen to how it sings, how it bends under the weight of the line, an easy, easy stroke, each time a little longer, feeling it a bit more, the rod bending and the line extending—until—you're—*there!*" And with this she brought the rod forward one last time, the curled line whipping above her head, out straight and beautiful, and then down softly in the dust of the runway. "Like I said, it's all rhythm," she said and smiled. "Understand?"

"I guess."

"Good, so here's what I want you to do. Watch the way I hold it, not too tight or you'll lose the feel of it. I'll play out a little line with my free hand." She spooled one, then another, then a third arm's length of fishing line out onto the ground. "Now come on behind me, reach around and take hold of the rod with me."

I did as I was told, standing behind her with my right hand on hers, the sun-bronzed skin of her arm warm against mine.

"I'll worry about the line for now," she said. "All I want you to do is to get a feel for the rhythm of the rod. Ready?"

"Ready."

She brought her arm and shoulder back with a twist of her waist. The rod responded as if alive, the line jumping up off the ground and singing out as it swished by overhead. "Feel it now," she said as she maneuvered the rod backward and forward, backward and forward, the line curving beautifully, dancing silver in the sun under her touch and my own. I felt it all—the motion, neither slow nor rushed, the gentle pull of the played-out line at either end of the two-beat cycle, the subtle pause necessary for the line to catch and pass the extended tip of the rod. "Not too much wrist, or you'll whip it and tie a knot. That was your problem before. You getting it?"

"I think so."

"Ready for more?"

"Ready."

She played out more line. "So now we're building up to something. We're going to slow down the motion a bit, let the longer line catch up. Slowing some more now, but we've got to be stronger with the rod to keep up—feel it? See that pebble out there? That's our target. We're going to need a little more. Follow, follow—"

I could feel her tightened muscles, the firm, hard strokes of her arm. It seemed as if I had become an extension of her, all sense of space absent between us as we moved together, shoulder on shoulder, skin on skin, a *pas de deux* on that dusty runway. "One, two, three—*release.*" Our arms came forward and then stopped, the tip of the rod pointed towards the small pebble, line swishing past one last time then out and out, arching forward and drifting down, landing about half an inch short of the mark. We stood there for a moment longer, my arm draped around her shoulder, my hand still holding hers on the extended pole. She glanced back at me and smiled. "Close enough," she said. "Now try it yourself."

I practiced for a while as Kathy watched, cautioning me about too loose a wrist, correcting me when I brought the rod back too far, or held it out at too flat an angle, or pointed the tip too low on release. I felt like I was really getting it when I heard the drone of the approaching plane. "We better clear out before we get run over," I said and reeled in the line. "You going to wake up your friend?"

"Angie's not asleep, just soaking in rays." As if on cue, Angie stood up, snatched her shirt from the grass and sauntered to safety, sweat beads glistening on her chest and tightly toned stomach.

The plane banked low, curving gracefully in the broad, blue sky. We detoured out to the narrow path along the fence, a safe distance from the runway. "Where did you learn how to do all that?" I asked.

Kathy walked on silently for a few moments. "My dad," she finally said, her words spoken as a near-whisper, barely audible over the whine of the approaching plane. "My dad—and my brother—and—it's kind of a long story."

"I've got time."

"Not now."

"Too bad they couldn't come along. Too busy?"

"Something like that."

"What do they do?"

The plane's engine was nearly deafening. We turned just as the tires scuffed the ground, sending up a plume of dust. It hurtled down the runway before stopping in another wrenching spin. "They were investment bankers," Kathy said. "They worked together, in the same office." The use of the past tense seemed strange to me. Fired, perhaps, or gone onto another line of work? As I wondered about this, her eyes focused on my own. "At Cantor Fitzgerald," she said.

Cantor Fitzgerald. The words tumbled through my mind. The way she said it made me understand. Cantor's office was in the North Tower of the World Trade Center. Nearly everyone lost after the plane hit on 9/11. *"Kind of a long story."* From her expression, I knew that she knew I understood. She reached out, gave my hand a squeeze, and set out across the runway toward her friend.

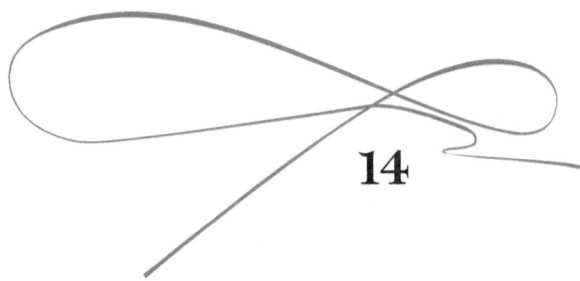

14

The plane carrying Kathy and Angie had barely disappeared before I began to feel uncomfortable in my resting place atop the stacked palettes, but it wasn't the heat of the Alaskan summer sun that was getting to me. Although many years had passed since 9/11, the idea that Kathy's father and brother had just begun another day's work on that beautiful September morning when the planes struck the towers— images of them vanishing with the others, obliterated in the collapse and conflagration—brought back vivid, visceral memories of that horrific day and left me feeling sick.

I hopped down off the stack and leaned back against it, nestling within a sliver of shade thrown by the palettes. I tried reading but my mind continued to wander, my eyes absentmindedly scanning the pages. I set the book down and pulled out my notebook and pen, continuing the travel log I had first started in the Anchorage airport.

A short time later Zack came over. I glanced up at him, his mass of unruly hair and beard glowing in the bright Alaskan sun. "Writin' somethin'?" he said.

"Just taking some notes."

"About the trip?"

"Yeah. A journal."

"You got a name for it?"

"I don't know. Maybe something like *Larry and David's Excellent Adventure in Alaska.*"

"Sounds cool."

"Actually, that one's already been taken, sort of. Tell you what, how about you come up with a better name and let me know."

"Damn, Doc, it's your goddamn book, I ain't goin' to name it for you. Anyways, seems like you already got a lot to write about," he said and laughed. "I mean, all that bullshit with the hunters yesterday..." He didn't bother to finish the sentence, just standing there shaking his head and smiling that way people smile about things that are beyond belief.

"Tell me about it," I said. "I'm just trying to jot down the key bits and pieces that'll bring back bigger memories later. Otherwise, I'll fall behind and then I'll never finish, and all kinds of good stuff will get left out."

Zack sat down on the weeds and gravel in front of me. "I'll tell you something if you promise not to tell anybody else. I've always wanted to be a writer."

This was unexpected. "A writer?"

"You sound surprised. You don't think I can write or somethin'?"

"Anyone can write," I said. "So, what kind of writing are you interested in? Short stories? Creative nonfiction? Young adult novels?"

He looked at me like I was speaking in tongues. "Shit, all I really want to do is write songs for a rock band. Classic stuff. You know, something like 'Layla' or maybe 'Stairway to Heaven'." He closed his eyes and sang out the last few bars of the latter with an intensity that looked like he was praying. Although his key was flat, I couldn't help but appreciate the sincerity, as well as his interest in songs that were considered ancient even by my generation.

I closed my notebook, stretched, stood. Zack sprung to his feet and brushed the pebbles from his thighs. "I can't be much help to you when it comes to rock lyrics," I said, "but it sounds to me like what you're really interested in is poetry."

"*Poetry*?"

"Yeah. Songs are just poems, put to music. The great song-writers really are great poets to begin with: John Lennon, Bob Dylan, Joni Mitchell—"

"Gregg Allman?"

"Absolutely."

"So, what do you know about poetry?"

Truth is, I didn't know much about it at all. I always wanted to, though. It seemed like a marvelous means of creative expression, well-tailored to a lifestyle like mine that didn't permit sufficient blocks of time to work on longer pieces. "It's really not all that hard. You just need to think of something you want to write about, but instead of writing a big story, try to dig down deep and use just a sparing selection of words to capture its essence."

"*Huh*?"

"Let's try it this way. See that building over there, where we picked up the luggage?"

"Where I almost killed those fuckin' hunters?"

"Yeah, exactly. Let me try to come up with a short poem about it."

"About that crappy old building with the hole in the side?"

"Sure, why not?"

"Shit, even Gregg Allman couldn't write a poem about that."

"Maybe not, but I'll give it a shot anyway." I hesitated, head down, running my fingers through my hair. And then—

We stand inside, waiting,
Peering through the hole in the wall
Like a dentist looking in his patient's mouth.
We see nothing. And then it seems
As if the mouth is smiling
At a joke all its own. A secret
Kept from us, that will bring us
Only sorrow.

"There," I said. "How's that?"

"That's a poem?"

"Kind of."

"It's pretty shitty, if you don't mind me sayin'."

"I know it was a shitty poem. I was just trying to show you—"

"I mean, it didn't even rhyme. Ain't a poem got to rhyme?"

"Not always, no."

"What the hell kind of poem is it that don't rhyme?"

"It's called—never mind. You're right, it was a shitty poem. I'm sure you could do better."

"Damn right, and mine would rhyme."

"Tell you what. Take this—" I ripped a page from my notebook and handed it to him. "And here's a pen."

"You're giving me your *pen?*"

"Don't worry about it. Do me a favor, though, and don't tell your dad, because I know it wasn't on his packing list. I brought a couple more with me, just in case."

"I ain't sayin' a thing."

"Good. Now go write yourself a poem."

"And you'll read it?"

"Only if you want me to."

"What should I write about?"

"Anything."

"Seriously? Anything?"

I could see by the lost look in his eyes that the assignment had to be narrowed a bit. "Just describe something—Nalunaq, the plane ride, the river, Alaska—whatever you want. You can also try putting down some thoughts about people—"

"Like my dad or my brother?"

"Exactly."

"Maybe even my mom, but I barely remember her. Butch remembers her some."

"She's not alive?"

"No. Died a long time ago."

"Sorry to hear that. Just put down some of the things you do remember and build around them. That's the great thing about poetry. You can make it all up, straight out of your heart."

He pondered this for a moment, and then it seemed like something just clicked. "So that's what you mean by *essence*?"

"Exactly!"

Zack stuck out his fist and I bumped mine against it. "Shit, maybe I was cut out for poetry after all. I'll find you when I'm ready."

"I'll look forward to it," I said, and felt like I really meant it.

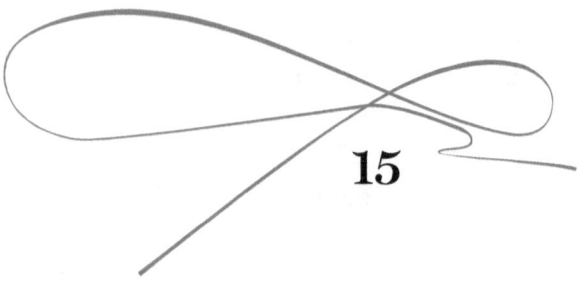

15

Zack and I heard the distant whine of the plane making its final return and went to find Larry. He lay on his back, his dog-eared copy of *Fisherman's World* draped over his face. "Our turn," I said and nudged the bottom of his sneakered foot. "We're heading out."

Larry jumped to his feet and glanced at his watch. "Jesus, one-thirty already! Half the day's gone! We're missing good fishing time!"

Zack shielded his eyes and sighted the approaching plane. "I wouldn't worry about it," he said. "It's been cold and rainy out here for the past coupla weeks. I'm hopin' that fog yesterday was the end of it. Fish don't seem all that hungry when the weather turns cold. Looks like you timed it just right, they're probably near starvin'. I'll bet they'll go for just about anything you throw at 'em today."

"Is the fishing really going to be that good?" Larry said.

"Should be if the weather holds up."

I could sense my brother's agitation, borne of expectancy and the possibility of soon-to-be fulfilled dreams. I hoped it would begin to wash away the fear and pain endured during his cancer treatment and then our dad's death, saddling Larry with running a business I only now began to realize he found more confining than a solitary cell in some supermax prison. I hoped that Zack was right about how hungry the fish were going to be. I didn't want to think about Larry having to endure another disappointment. "Are they already fishing out there?" Larry asked. I sensed he was ready to charge the plane as soon as its wheels hit the ground.

"Don't you worry, no one's doing any fishing until we all get there," Zack said. "There's a ton of work that needs to be done before anybody puts a line in. Just count yourself lucky that most of it'll be done by the time we land."

The plane skidded to a stop. Luke LaDue jumped out of the pilot's door. "Okay, let's get this puppy loaded up," he shouted and opened the cargo hatch. Zack, Larry, and I worked fast, stowing away the remaining gear. "Get yourselves in," LaDue said as he shut the hatch. "Two in the back, one up front with me."

LaDue climbed into the pilot seat, closed his door, slipped his radio headset on over his ears. Zack was first in through the passenger door. "I hate these fucking flights," he said as he squeezed himself into the back. "They make me sick to my stomach."

I intended to follow Zack, but Larry took hold of my shoulder. "Bro, you want to sit up front? You got it."

"You sure?"

"You saved this whole goddamn trip. The front seat's yours." He climbed in and settled into the back seat alongside Zack.

We took off to the east and banked sharply south, following the Nalunaq River just below. The village seemed to disappear in an instant, swallowed by the immensity of the surrounding wilderness, the surprisingly flat land below us dotted with countless ponds and lakes. I was expecting forest, but the only trees grew in a thin line, curtain-like along the river. "Dat dere's part of the largest delta in the world," Luke LaDue shouted over the drone of the engine. "Permafrost. Only the top few feet melt in the summer. 'Cause it's frozen beneath, the water ain't got no place to go." And then he paused and looked at me with an expression more serious than I'd imagined him capable of. "At least, dat's the way it used to be."

He paused again, seeming to be sizing me up, assessing with his eyes whether this last comment of his was a throw-away as far as I was concerned or, perhaps, not. I responded with a quizzical look, and this apparently was enough. He banked the plane to the left, heading west-southwest as best as I could tell. In a minute or two we were over some power lines that seemed to stretch forever to the horizon. He pointed to them then dropped altitude and straightened the plane, putting them more clearly in my view. From this lower vantage point, I could see that what had appeared to be a straight line was anything but; most of the poles were listing far to the south and east, some looking as if the electric cables strung from the crosspieces at their tops were all that was keeping them from falling over. "When I first started flyin' up here, dem poles were straight," he shouted. "Bottoms anchored in solid ice. Only it ain't so solid no more. All melting down below, movin' northwest, like the river. A few years more, dey'll be down, count on it."

He pulled back on his control stick, throwing the plane into a gut-twisting ascent while turning back to our former course. "How long have you been up here?" I asked after my stomach had settled back beneath my diaphragm.

"Six years now, goin' on seven."

"Those poles were straight only six years ago?"

"As an arrow. I was born and raised in Louisiana, if you couldn't guess. Little town out on the bayou. Place called Houma, about sixty miles southwest of New Orleans. Ever heard of it?" I shook my head. "Didn't think so. Anyways, after Katrina, I figure Houma ain't got much of a future. So, I figure, I got to get as far away from Louisiana as I can, but I don't want to go no place foreign, being an American citizen and all. I look on a map and I figure Alaska's about a far away as I can get, pack up my wife and little girl and move up here. Only now I see that things are about as fucked up here as down there—pardon my French."

"No problem."

"Came up here not too long after gettin' back from Iraq. Moved to a little village not too much bigger than Nalunaq. My daughter was ten when we left. Grew up here." A look of sadness flashed across his face. "She's gone now."

"Gone?"

"Yeah, back to the lower forty-eight."

"Where?"

"Don't know for sure. Anyways, she ain't never comin' back here again, least that's what she said before she left. Tell you somethin', life up here has its disadvantages."

We left the flatlands behind and passed over some high hills. Some of the brown, bare ridges were scarred with narrow paths, routes of caribou herds that traverse this region, LaDue explained. He pointed ahead to his right and tilted my side down for a better look. A grizzly lumbered along the path atop the approaching ridge, followed by three cubs. "That's why it's against the law to hunt by plane," he shouted. "Too goddamn easy."

He banked the plane around to the east at a point where a shallow tributary joined with the broader, island-studded river we'd been following, the junction marked by a patch of white water. He turned the plane to follow the smaller river. Once again, he pointed and began to shout. "That's what you'll be fishin' on."

Gazing down at it I felt vaguely disappointed. I had imagined spending the week floating down a broad, majestic river surrounded by a heavily forested wilderness. This looked more like a common stream in what appeared to be mostly open land once you got past the thicket of trees and underbrush snaking alongside near the water's edge. Still, the image of the grizzly and her cubs wandering along that naked ridgetop served as a useful reminder that our view below was not one of a greatly expanded neighborhood park. "What's it called?" I said. He pointed to his headset and shook his head, "The river," I shouted. "What's the name of the river down there?"

Before LaDue could answer, Zack's hand landed on my shoulder. He leaned forward in his seat, his other hand resting alongside the pilot's neck. "Don't tell him, Luke," he shouted, then turned towards me. "Sorry, Doc, but he can't tell you. It's part of the deal with my dad."

"Wiley's the only guide around who uses this river," LaDue said. "Most of the guides use the Salmon River. They've got a nice, wide landing strip at the put-in. Easy to fly into."

"Too easy," Zack said. "Too many people. Ain't wilderness if there's other people all around, at least that's what my dad says."

I twisted in my seat so Zack could hear me. "So, if I want to tell people back home the name of the river we fished on, what do I say?"

Zack shrugged. "I don't know, tell 'em it's a secret. I guess you could tell 'em you fished on the Secret River."

"The Secret River?" Larry said. "Never heard of it."

"'Cause I just made it up," Zack said.

LaDue pointed out the windshield. "Check that out," he said. A moose stood in a shallow valley between ridges. Luke nosed the plane down, close enough to make out the huge set of antlers on the magnificent beast as we flew over. "Largest rack I've seen this year."

After flying over one more row of hills, Luke LaDue throttled down the engine. I scanned in all directions but saw nothing except a small, flat valley leading to another row of brown-sided hills, and the Secret River, a picturesque but otherwise inconsequential stream just below us. We descended to around three hundred feet, and I noticed a shack at the far end of the valley, perched on a river-carved promontory at the base of the next range of hills. A thin, orange strip lay just to the right of the cabin, a scratch upon the otherwise unspoiled land. Like the cabin alongside, it was bordered on three sides by small cliffs. "Tray tables in their upright and locked positions," he said. "And hold the hell on!"

We hit the ground harder than I imagined it was possible for the plane to survive. Luke braked and spun the tail just before we reached the drop-off at the end of the runway, kicking up a thick, orange dust cloud. Now I understood what he was practicing for back at Nalunaq. "You boys are lucky," LaDue said. "Dat dere was my best landing today."

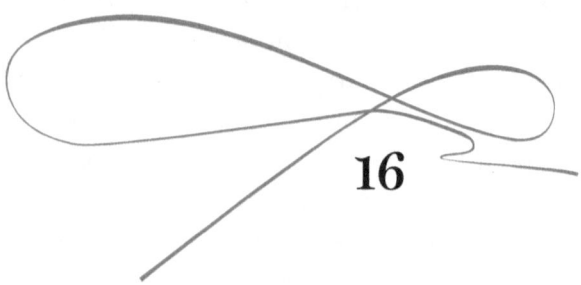

16

A sharp, fingers-in-mouth whistle sounded from across the river. "Let's go!" Wiley cried out. "We gotta get moving!"

Larry grabbed his bag and hurried down the slope. I paused for a moment, fighting a sense of foreboding as I watched the plane lift off and disappear. Pelts of wolf and bear draped the sides of the cabin next to the runway, flattened heads with open, wild-toothed mouths and dazed, dead eyes. Their dangling legs with sharp-clawed paws flapped in the breeze, tapping against the sides of the cabin as if sounding out a message in code, a vow of revenge, a warning against further advance into a land more theirs than ours.

"Ain't never seen no one here in all the years we've been usin' this strip," Zack said. "But the pelts keep changin', so them hunters gotta be out there somewheres."

I took big, sliding steps down the gravelly slope, stopping at the edge of a marsh. "Gotta get into your waders," Zack said. "You might think about ditchin' them shorts and puttin' on some long pants underneath. That water's pretty cold."

I dug the waterproof overalls out of my bag. Larry already had his on so I ignored Zack's advice and slid them over my shorts, the rubberized cloth cold against my bare legs. I slipped the sealed feet over heavy woolen socks, tied on the wading boots Larry had given me and put on Larry's old fly-fishing vest. "Looking good," Larry said. "Too bad Dad's not around to see this. He wouldn't believe it."

I lifted my waterproof duffel high over my head and followed Larry and Zack into the frigid waters of the Secret River. I slogged through the marsh, sinking deeper and deeper, the river lapping at the top of my waders, threatening to spill down my chest. I managed to stay dry but regretted that I didn't follow Zack's advice to change out of my shorts. I could barely make my way up the opposite bank with the numbness in my feet.

I was shivering hard as I emerged from the river. "Jesus, David, you look near frozen," Kathy said, standing warm and comfortable in her thick down coat.

"Near?" I said.

"Here, take this." Kathy unzipped her coat and held it out to me. I hesitated. "Please take it," she said. "Not smart to get hypothermic on our first day." I draped her coat over my shoulders and pulled it tight around me, the comforting warmth soon taking an edge off my shivering.

Wiley clapped his hands. "Okay, now, listen up," he shouted. "It's four to a raft, not including me, Zack and Butch. Don't worry about who you're with. They'll be plenty of chances to switch up later if you want to. Let's move!"

I returned Kathy's coat and put on my ski jacket, thinking it hard to believe that I needed it in August. I thought Kathy might want to ride with me, but she followed Angie over to Butch's raft. Larry and Carl Cooper hovered near Babcock, maneuvering to see who could snatch the seat alongside him. Larry proved quicker, hurdling the girdle of the raft to capture the coveted spot. Since Tony Giordano and Tyler Babcock traveled as a team, Larry's claim to the seat alongside Babcock left only one vacancy. I assumed that Cooper would take it, but he shot Larry an angry look and headed off to sit with his buddies and Rick Garrett in the raft piloted by Wiley.

I settled into the last seat in Larry's raft. On a command from Zack, Larry and I pushed hard against the gravely bottom with our booted feet until we were floating free in the Secret River.

Although my practice sessions with Kathy had given me a rudimentary sense of how to cast, I hadn't had any instruction in tying the fly onto the fishing line. It was far more complicated than I imagined, involving a leader, or tippet—which can be a floating tippet or a sinking tippet depending on what you're fishing for—that's tied to the main fishing line with one of a variety of knots. Larry's favorite was a nail knot, which doesn't actually use a nail but instead involves a small segment of hollow plastic straw around which the fly line is looped and then threaded. Larry showed me as we began our float downstream, murmuring how stupid he was for not teaching me this while on land, particularly since his taking time to instruct me meant that he was the last to have his fly in the water. It didn't help when Carl Cooper's whooping announced the first strike. "The fucker must have a silver," Larry murmured as he tied on my tippet, wound it and my fishing line together around the straw and through its hollow center, moistened the line with saliva and pulled the knot tight.

"Ain't no silvers this high up," Babcock reassured him. "Got to wait a coupla days before we hit salmon. Right now, we'll be fishin' for Arctic char, maybe a Dolly Varden. Rainbows are a possibility, except you ain't seen anything jumping, and rainbows just love to jump." None of this mattered to Larry. Everyone else already had their lines in the river except for him and me, and the way he looked while he fumbled to finish the nail knot made it clear that, from now on, I'd be responsible for tying on my own tippets. Babcock's words proved prescient when a disappointed Carl Cooper lifted a baby char no bigger than an oversized sardine from the river.

With my line and leader finally prepared, I followed Babcock's advice, chose one of Larry's salmon egg flies and tied it on with a clinch knot (with Tony's help). I felt nervous, fearing that, despite the practice session with Kathy, my first attempt at casting would be more likely to impale one of my raft mates than catch a fish. And God help me if I caught something before Larry did.

And so I waited, the fly dangling in the soft breeze while Tony hauled in two beautiful, orange-bellied Dolly Vardens, releasing them gently back into the river in accordance with Wiley's demand that no fish be harmed during the trip. I waited while Babcock hooked a beautiful rainbow trout that burst from the river in a series of spectacular jumps, arching and twisting high over the water before splashing back down. I waited while Larry cast and cast and cast again, only to have the fly return to the raft wet and empty. From time to time, Babcock would glance at Larry, looking pained at his inability to hook anything, then back at me, perplexed at the salmon ball fly dangling dry from the tip of the pole resting by my side. After a while, Babcock rested his rod between his meaty thighs and turned towards me. "Doc," he said, "you want to know lesson A-number-one of fishin'?"

"What's that?" I said.

"It's one hundred ten percent impossible to catch anything but a cold unless you put your line in the water. Guarantee it."

I nodded my appreciation, lifted my rod, pulled out some slack with my left hand, and with great care brought the rod back over my right shoulder. The line responded and the fly followed, sailing up into surprisingly graceful flight. Forward and back—two, three, four times—and then one last strong reach forward, just as Kathy had taught me. Larry's faux salmon eggs plopped down on the surface, spun a bit with the current, disappeared.

The next sensation sent my heart into my throat. A snag. Please, God, let this be a snag. Tyler Babcock's cry ended all such hope. "Set the hook, Doc! You got a live one!"

I flicked the rod back with my wrist. The pole bent into a hairpin as the line whizzed from the reel. "Looks like a Dolly," Babcock said. "Good-sized one, too." I played the fish as he instructed, the tip of my rod following the fish's desperate moves to free itself, allowing the line to run during its frantic attempts at escape, reeling the line back in when the fish rested. Before long I had it up near the boat, its blazing red back and bright orange spots flashing beautiful in the icy clear water. Zack laid down his oars, clambered over the stowed gear with net in hand, and scooped the exhausted fish from the river. "It's a beauty," he said as he untangled the fins from the netting, removed the hook, and held it up before him lengthwise in the classic fisherman's trophy pose. "This baby's yours," he said, and held the fish out toward me.

Normally I'm not squeamish. During my medical training, I'd held an amputated leg from a drunk who fell into the path of the Number 4 Express on the Lexington line; bits of brain falling from an open skull wound suffered by some guy from

Alphabet City hit by a speeding delivery van while attempting a midnight dash across the FDR Drive; and a variety of internal organs, including the hearts, lungs, and livers of adults and children drifting in that strange, unknowable dimension between life and death. There was nothing that should have made me hesitate to take hold of my trophy. And yet I did hesitate. Perhaps it was because of a distant memory, the time when, as a boy fishing with Larry and my father in a local pond, I was stabbed by the tip of the dorsal fin of a small perch I had caught. Perhaps I harbored a subconscious aversion to fish slime. Most likely, it was because I didn't want to make a big deal of this with Larry remaining fishless. Whatever the reason, I had about as much intention of taking hold of that fish than I would have a downed, smoking power line. Then I heard a "*woo-hoo!*" from across the river and saw Kathy standing up on her raft, waving her arms above her head. "Great catch!" she shouted. "What is it?"

"Got me a Dolly—?" I glanced over at Babcock.

"Dolly Varden," he said.

"A Dolly Varden," I shouted.

Kathy flashed me two thumbs up. "Beautiful! Make sure you get a picture."

Right. A picture. Tony pulled a camera from a pocket of his fishing vest. "Say '*plastics*'," he said.

With Tony pointing his camera at me and Kathy cheering me on from across the river, I had little choice but to take hold of my fish. I held it as Zack had held it, gently enough not to harm it but firmly enough to prevent its escape. Rather than being repulsed by the feel of it, I couldn't help but marvel at its strength and power. Sleek, firm muscle, a beautiful swimming machine; holding it, I could only begin to imagine the hundreds, perhaps thousands of miles it had swum in its cycle of birth, growth, and reproduction. "You got yourself a nice male there," Babcock said. "You can tell by the hooked mouth, the red back and bright orange spots. Mating colors. Better put that sucker back so it can go fertilize some eggs before it dies. Hate to have it swim all this way for nothin'."

Tony took the picture. I bent over the side and set the fish gently into the water. It floated listless until the cold water revived it. It flicked its tail and disappeared back into the river. "Gotta love them Dollys," Babcock said as he sent his line soaring. "Just about the prettiest fish going, if you ask me."

We fished on, floating down the river beneath a beautiful afternoon sky now dappled with high white clouds. Tony pulled in a couple of nice rainbows, Babcock netted a Dolly more colorful than my own, Kathy hooked onto a monster of a rainbow trout. Even Angie caught something, shrieking in delight as she reeled in an Arctic char.

Only Larry remained without a catch. I could sense his fury as he let his line fly, higher and further than I had seen anyone cast a line before. A moment later his line bent under a strike. Babcock sounded as relieved as I felt. "Pull him in, there," he coached. "You got him good now, just bring him on in."

Larry brought the fish home with a few quick turns of his wrist; a decent sized Arctic char. He lifted it from the water, removed the hook and set it back into the river.

We fished for another three hours before reaching the beach that Wiley used for his first night of camping. We grounded the rafts and hauled off the supplies and tents. Butch and Zack set up three double-burner camp stoves alongside the bear barrels containing dinner and our breakfast for the next morning. Butch lit the stoves and began cooking while Zack roamed the campsite, offering help setting up tents.

Everyone but Wiley slept two to a tent. For the most part, the sleeping arrangements were straightforward: Babcock and Tony, Russ and Bob Billings, Kathy and Angie, Larry and me. Only Garrett came alone on the trip. Wiley took the three Nashville guys aside and said that one of them had to share a tent with Garrett. An intense discussion ended with a tense round of "rock, paper, scissors." Cooper lost, kicking at the sand and storming off down the beach.

Zack approached Larry and me as we began to unpack our tent. We'd chosen a spot that seemed relatively private, away from the river near the edge of the thick underbrush. "You don't want to put down here," he said.

"Looks good to me," Larry said. "What's wrong with it?"

"See that right there?" Zack gestured to a sandy trail heading off through dense, shoulder-high bushes. "That's the way to the bathroom. Too much traffic, and it might get to smellin'."

Zack found us a different spot down a little way, next to a narrow stream gurgling along its rocky route across the beach before flowing into the river. "This is about as far out as you want to get, what with the grizzlies and wolves," he said.

"Do they know that?" I nodded further down the beach where Kathy and Angie had laid out their ground cloth.

"What the hell?" Zack leapt the stream and trotted the twenty or so yards out to them. As Larry and I set up our tent, their conversation reached me on the breeze. "We girls need our privacy," Angie said. "Butch said it would be all right."

"If he thinks we should be closer—" Kathy began, but she didn't have a chance against Angie's determination to stay right there.

"Butch said we're good here," Angie said. "Come on, Kathy, let's get this set up." She unpacked the tent and spread it over the ground cloth.

"I hope some wolf takes that chick out," Zack said as he strode past us, back to where his brother's minute steaks filled the air with the delicious scent of grilling meat. As I looked over at Butch, grinning through his beard as he worked his spatula amid the flames spitting from the grill, I couldn't help but think that Zack might get his wish.

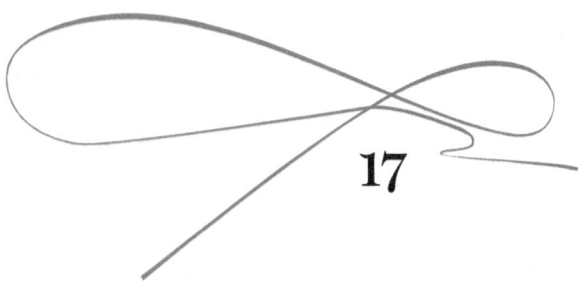

17

After our dinner of minute steak sandwiches, instant mashed potatoes, and lemon pound cake, I sat atop a log, sipping a steaming mug of coffee. I felt chilled despite my winter-weight long underwear, jeans, turtleneck, insulated vest, and ski jacket; I looked forward to zipping myself inside the down sleeping bag awaiting me in my tent. A shiver pulsed through me as I watched Larry, Babcock, Cooper, and a few others finish their dinner still wearing their wet gear. These were the hardest of the hardcore fishermen, a group for whom dinner was just a necessary interruption in time better spent with their lines in the water.

Wiley appeared holding a six-foot metal stake, a tattered piece of yellow cloth tied to its top. His other hand gripped the handles of two small shovels, the types used by infantry to dig foxholes. "Ladies and gentlemen," he called out, "one last but important piece of business. This here pole marks the entrance to the camp restrooms. You all watch where Zack puts it, so you can find it in the dark. If you need to go, you go there. I don't want you all foulin' up the whole beach." Zack took the pole, loped down the beach to the trail between the bushes he'd pointed out to Larry and me, and jammed it into the ground. "Seeing that we've got ladies on the trip, we've got two bathroom areas set up," Wiley said as Zack jogged back and stood by my side. "The ladies' room is on the left of the trail, men's on the right. Remember, *ladies on the left*—you all got that? Use these here shovels to dig a hole to do your business. Now, about those matches I told you all to put in a plastic bag along with your toilet paper? When you're done, you light up a match and burn the paper. You got that?"

"Why the hell we need to burn our toilet paper?" Carl Cooper asked.

"Why the hell? 'Cause we got some big old bears out there that love the smell of toilet paper, that's why. And I don't want them bears coming around and digging up what we leave behind, 'cause it'll turn this place into a stinking mess. Any other questions? No? Good. I brought two shovels, one for the boys' room and one for the girls'." Wiley stuck one shovel point down into the sand, searched through the many pockets on his fishing vest before finding a blue ribbon deep inside the pocket above the right side of his chest and tied it around the handle of the shovel he still held. "This here's the lady's shovel," he said.

"Ain't a lady's shovel supposed to have a pink ribbon?" Butch said and winked at Angie.

"Tell you what, mister smart aleck," Wiley said. "Shoot your mouth off one more time and I'm goin' to have you do the diggin' for these here good people with your own two hands."

"My dickhead brother probably would, at least for that Angie chick," Zack whispered to me. "Pisses my dad off something fierce when he goes after ladies on our trips."

"Not sure who's going after whom," I said.

"I'm heading to bed," Wiley said. "You all should think

about doing the same. It's been a long day, and we're getting an early start tomorrow."

Wiley headed over toward the bathroom trail carrying the shovels. He stuck the ribboned one in the sand and disappeared into the bushes carrying the other. "Like a fucking clock," Zack said. And then, something entirely unexpected. "Guess what, Doc? Wrote my first poem. Mind if I find you after cleanup and read it?"

My plan was to crawl into my tent alongside Larry, zip up inside my warm sleeping bag, read a page or two of John McPhee, and fall dead asleep. The Larry part of that idea fizzled out when he grabbed his pole and flies and headed down to the river with Babcock, Cooper, and the other crazies, evidently planning to fish until it got dark, which wouldn't happen until sometime after midnight. Maybe he'd have a shot at seeing the northern lights, I figured, the only reason I could think of to be sorry that I wasn't going with him. "Sure," I said to Zack. "Be happy to. Need a hand with kitchen cleanup?"

"Thanks, we got it covered. Besides, looks like we already got some help." He nodded back toward the kitchen. Butch washed the plastic plates, cups, and utensils in a rubber bucket filled with steaming, soapy water, dunked them in the rinse bucket alongside and handed them to Angie, who dried them as fast as Butch could wash them. "Looks like they make a good team," I said.

"Yeah, well, we'll see how long that lasts," Zack said. "I'll find you when I'm done."

Kathy came over moments after Zack left. "Want to check out our digs?" she said. We jumped the little stream together and headed toward her tent. As we drew closer, I caught the scent of something smoky, pungent, exotic. She unzipped the screen mesh. A stick of incense stood in a ceramic holder in the near corner of the tent alongside the foot of Angie's sleeping bag, a curling trail of smoke drifting up from its glowing tip.

"Burning incense in a closed tent?" I said.

"Angie's idea," Kathy offered.

"You guys are going to asphyxiate in there, if the tent doesn't burn down first."

"I raised that issue with her."

"And?"

"She promised me it would be okay."

"She *promised you*?"

"Okay, it's not the best idea. We were roomies in college, I've seen her do crazier things."

I backed away from the tent and took a reviving breath of chilly Alaskan air. "Angie went to *Princeton*?"

"*Phi beta kappa*. Graduated *magna cum laude*. Better than I did."

"You guys just seem so different."

"Sometimes different can be good, don't you think?"

I took another deep breath, coughed out more fumes of smoky incense. I could taste it in my mouth. "Definitely," I said.

Kathy smiled and planted a kiss on my cheek. "You think you and I are different?" she said.

"How the hell should I know?" I said. "We only met about a day ago. Besides, you're the psychologist. What do you think?"

"I think you're a good person, doctor David—what is your last name again?"

"Nichols."

"Nichols—right. Like the coins. Now I won't forget."

"Spelled differently."

"I kinda guessed that. Come on."

She took my hand. We walked past her tent and sat down on the dry gravel of the high riverbank. We'd left the camp behind; here there was only the gentle rippling of the river over rocky shallows and rotting logs, the timeless river-scent heavy on the chill breeze. Kathy nestled closer. "Your brother's quite the fisherman," she said.

"That he is."

"You never got the bug?"

"Guess not. Hobbies were never my thing."

"I've seen you writing."

"Just a journal. A reminder of my day-to-day. An arrogant attempt to ensure my immortality to future generations who might read this tripe. Chasing after wind."

"Ecclesiastes."

"Beautiful book," I said. "Whoever the author was must have been a genius."

"And clinically depressed."

"They were short on antidepressants in his day. Lucky for us."

"Some scholars think it was written by a woman."

"Okay. Her day."

A shout echoed from down the river; someone had caught something. I hoped it was Larry. "Too busy for hobbies?" Kathy said. "Really?"

"My job keeps me pretty busy, but I'm not complaining."

"What, exactly, do you do again?"

"You really want to go into this?"

"I wouldn't have asked if I didn't."

"It's like I said before, I study cell death. *Apoptosis*— remember?"

"Right, apoptosis. Hard word to remember."

"Not one that comes up often in general conversation."

"Not between normal people." She smiled, gave me a nudge. "So, let me ask you a question at the risk of exposing my basic ignorance. What's there to it? I mean, cells die. Big deal, right?"

"Not exactly. Most cells have figured out how to die in a highly organized way. When a cell ages or is damaged beyond survivability, or is infected with something bad, the apoptotic enzyme cascade is triggered and the cell dies."

"Cell suicide."

"Pretty much." Kathy closed her eyes, shook her head.

"What is it?" I said.

"I was just thinking of millions of tiny cells marching around with suicide vests on, waiting to go *blam!*"

"Kind of sick," I said and smiled. "But it's actually the opposite. It's controlled death. Organized. The cell breaks apart, with its key components repackaged and available for future use."

"Cellular recycling."

"Exactly. If cells went *blam*, they'd spill their guts into your blood stream in a totally uncontrolled way. If that happens, and sometimes it does, you'd get big problems. If enough of them die that way all at once—"

I stopped my thought when I heard Zack calling my name. I motioned with a finger to my lips for Kathy to stay quiet. "You're not going to answer him?" she whispered. I shushed her and shook my head.

Kathy twisted in the direction of the call, her hands cupped around her lips. "David's over here," she shouted.

"What the hell?" I whispered.

"He likes you. Be nice."

Zack's heavy boots crunched toward us on the gravel. "Here it is," Zack said. "My poem."

Kathy shot me a quizzical look. "Right—your poem," I said. "That's—that's great."

"I didn't know you wrote poetry," Kathy said.

"Just learnin'," Zack said. "Doc here said he'd help me."

"You write poetry, too?" Kathy said. "Another non-hobby?"

"It's not my specialty—"

"Doc told me he'd teach me to write poetry like Gregg Allman."

"No kidding," Kathy said, smiling at me. "You're simply *full* of surprises."

"Oh, yeah," Zack said. "He's real big into Gregg Allman."

"Well, I *love* Gregg Allman," Kathy gushed. "What've you got?"

I saw the sudden panic in Zack's eyes. "I was just plannin' on readin' it to Doc, here," he said. "You wanna hear it, too?"

"If you want it to be just between you boys, that's fine—"

Kathy made a move to stand. I placed my hand on her knee and pressed her back down. "It's useful to get more than one perspective when assessing a piece of art," I said.

Zack laughed. "Shit, this ain't no piece of art," he said. "It's just some stupid poem."

"No poem is stupid," Kathy said. "I'd love to hear it." I got up, pulled Kathy to her feet, dusted off my backside. Zack reached into a pocket of his cargo pants and removed the notebook paper I'd given him back in Nalunaq, now folded into a tight square. "Okay, then—here goes," he said as he shook the paper open. "This here poem's called *River Rider*."

"Appropriate for the setting," Kathy said. She took hold of my hand and squeezed.

Zack cleared his throat. "Okay. *River Rider*. Here goes." And then a long pause. He lowered the paper. "It's my first poem, y'all know."

"It'll be fine," Kathy said. "Just go for it."

"Right. Okay. 'River Rider.'"

> *I got a river, that needs ridin',*
> *And it flows damn near forever,*
> *And I don't know where it's goin',*
> *But I ain't gonna let it get me wet,*
> *I ain't gonna let it get*
> *This river rider.*

"How's that?"

I glanced over at Kathy, my teeth biting my lower lip.

"It's just my first one," Zack said.

"It's—it's really good," Kathy said. "Definitely Gregg Allman-esque."

"You could almost sing it," I added.

"You bet. You wanna hear?"

"Not necessary," I said. "I can hear it right up here," and tapped my head. Zack looked crestfallen. "All right," I said. "If you really want to sing it—"

"It ain't that, Doc."

"Then what's the problem?"

"That's the poem I always wanted to write. Not sure what to do next."

"Writer's block, huh?"

"I guess, if that's what you call it."

"Gregg Allman wrote more songs than *Midnight Rider*," Kathy said.

"Yeah, but his other stuff doesn't seem to work. Like, *Whippin' Post*. What the hell am I supposed to do with that? And *Jessica* ain't even got no words!" Zack crumpled up the paper and shoved it back into his pocket.

"I told you before that I'm not a real poet," I said. "But I can give you some advice, if you still want it."

"Shit yeah, Doc."

"My advice is that you stop trying to write like Gregg Allman. The world already has a Gregg Allman."

"Well, if it ain't Gregg Allman, then who?"

"You. Write like Zack Williams. The world only has one of those."

He lifted his head. "Ain't true, Doc. Back where I was growing up there was another Zack Williams in the grade behind me, only he was, like, the smartest kid in the class. A real nerd, if you know what I mean."

"I've met a few. But even if there's more than one guy named Zack Williams, there's only one of *you*. You need to write like you, not like anybody else."

"That ain't going to be easy."

"It never is."

"But even if I'm writing like me and not Gregg Allman, what do I write about?"

"About the things that are important," Kathy said. "Life. Love. Death. That'll keep you busy."

"Life, love, death," Zack said. "That's a lot to think about."

"Yes, it is," I said.

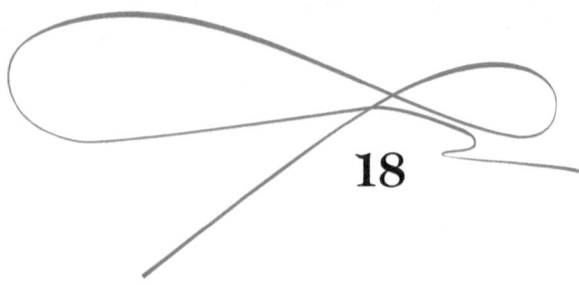

18

The rain started later that night, after darkness forced Larry and the others to put down their rods and return to their tents. The drumming on the rainfly awakened me, a new sound added to the night-song of the river rippling over rocks and logs. Larry remained asleep. We had slept in the same room virtually from the day I was born—two years and ten months after him—until I left for college eighteen years later. There was room enough in our house for each of us to have our own space, but our dad wouldn't have it. "I slept in the same bedroom with my brother until the war," he'd say by way of an explanation. I once tried to argue that he grew up in a two-bedroom apartment in Newark, New Jersey. We had four bedrooms. "That's not the point," he said.

It was only later that I began to understand what the point was, that after his own brother's death in the Battle of the Bulge, my father was grateful for every second they'd had together, including the time sleeping next to each other in their tiny Shephard Avenue apartment bedroom. The point being that, since none of us can know what the future holds, he wanted Larry and me to share the same bedroom until the time came for us to leave the house for good.

Larry's snoring made it difficult for me to return to sleep. Tina said it started after the radiation treatments to his neck. There were other side effects. Larry said he'd lost the feeling in his toes after the second round of chemo; he said it felt like his socks always were balled up in his shoes—nerve damage from one of the neurotoxic drugs in the regimen.

Larry rolled and stirred. "Caught a rainbow and two Dollys," he murmured. He pulled his sleeping bag high over his head and disappeared inside. My brother fished in his dreams.

I tried my best to fall back asleep. Perhaps I did, for a few moments at a time, but never long enough to really feel it. I gazed out the screened, rainfly-protected front flap, watching the beach and the bushes emerge in monochrome gray from the blackness of the brief Alaskan night, listening as the rain receded into a heavy night silence. At some point, the need to relieve myself forced me out of the tent.

I stood on the beach in my plastic camp sandals and long johns, feeling as if I had stepped into a black-and-white photograph. In the strange half-light, even the bright blue nylon of the tents seemed a dull gray. Swirls of thick fog arose from the water as if the damp breath of something alive.

I walked up to the marked pole and used the area behind the bushes designated for the men. Afterward, I glanced back at the camp, tent domes huddled against the river-bounded wilderness. I turned away as if in response to a call whispering through the gently swaying, mist-enshrouded tops of the cottonwoods. I headed further down the beach, crossed the little stream, and kept on past Kathy and Angie's tent, my arms folded across my chest and hands armpit-tucked against the chill. Mindful of Zack's warning about wolves and grizzlies, I headed down to the water's edge—as if that might help in an encounter with either.

I walked on, inhaling the cool air heavy with river-scent, treating my lungs to its life-affirming freshness after half a life spent breathing stale, recirculated laboratory air. I rounded the bend in the river, now out of sight of the camp. Completely alone. And then something caught my eye.

Up ahead, a shadowy figure stood in the river, half-cloaked within a swirling cloud of mist. A soft breeze passed, partially parting the shroud: Kathy, thigh-high in the water.

She crouched down, captured water in her cupped hands and doused herself, the water streaming over her hair and down her shoulders, back, breasts. She doused herself again, took in a deep breath and disappeared into the river, emerging a few moments later. She startled when she saw me, reflexively crouching back down into the river. She wiped her eyes and squinted through the morning gray. And then she stood, smiled, waved—an invitation.

I came closer, standing with my sandaled feet at the water's edge. A cold ripple splashed my toes. I stepped out of my sandals, pulled the bottoms of my long underwear above my calves, and stood ankle-high in the river. Within seconds, my feet went numb. "You're crazy," I said.

"Maybe," she said. "It's not so bad once you get used to it. C'mon."

I pulled my top over my head, balled it up and tossed it on the damp beach alongside Kathy's sweats, sandals, and towel. I took up some water, cupped it in my hand and splashed it up against the back of my neck. It felt as if an ice cube was sliding down my spine. I stuck my hands inside the waistband of my sweatpants, tugged—and then stopped. "I don't think so," I said.

She waved again. "It's refreshing."

"I—I can't" I said, hating myself for the words escaping my mouth. I slid my hands out from underneath the waistband and put my top back on. "Rain check?"

Kathy closed her eyes and ducked back down into the river. She remained beneath the surface for a long time before emerging, cascades of water flowing from her shoulders. "You sure?" she said.

"Yeah. Sorry."

She strode out of the river, picked up her towel and dried her goose-bumped skin. "It really wasn't bad," she said as she roughly toweled her hair. She stepped into her bottoms, came closer, rose up on tiptoes and kissed me, her lips cold and wet on mine. "About that rain check," she said. "I'll look forward to it." She pulled on her top and headed toward her tent.

I stood there, listening to the river, watching her cross the rocky beach and disappear into the mist. Wondering what the hell was wrong with me. Fighting the urge to strip off my clothes, walk into the frigid river, and float away.

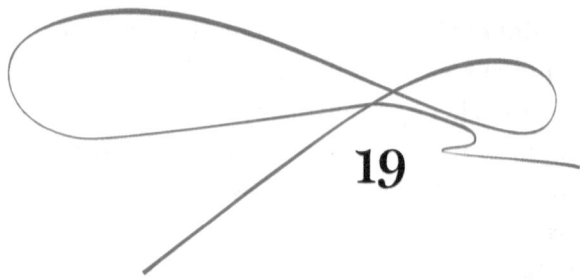

19

After a breakfast of bacon, eggs, and hot coffee, we changed back into our chest waders and boots, took down the tents, broke down the kitchen, and loaded the gear back into the rafts. The rain had long since passed but the gray chill remained. "Hope it clears up some," Zack said. "Otherwise we're going to have some sleepy fish, and when the fish are sleepy, the fishermen get ornery. Nothing worse than ornery fishermen on a fishing trip."

With the gear secure on the rafts, Wiley called us together for one last, peculiar ritual: 'walking the beach.' He spaced us evenly in a line extending from water's edge to the bushes, each of us an arm's length apart, and led us in a slow march from one end of the camp site to the other, searching for anything we might have left behind. As the line formed, I left my place near the end and slipped in alongside Kathy. "About this morning—"

"Nothing to worry about," Kathy said in a way that made me feel worse.

I had hoped that Larry and I would be joining Kathy and Angie. No such luck. We ended up with Carl Cooper along with his buddy, Paul Acer. Cooper climbed in first, pissing

Larry off by taking the prime casting seat at the back right of the raft. I tried to engage Cooper in conversation from my seat in the front, but I might as well have been talking to a rock. I came to understand that this was an angry fisherman, a fisherman likely to die with a rod in his hands. By the time we beached for the night, Cooper had managed to catch only one undersized grayling over the entire day.

The sky had cleared in the late afternoon; I hoped that we might see the northern lights that night. After dinner, more clouds drifted in, obscuring the stars and the waxing, three-quarter moon behind an iridescent curtain.

Once again, Larry was out fishing when I fell asleep. I awakened later with him alongside me, his head protruding from his zipped sleeping bag. His snoring kept me awake, so I decided to make use of the time and take advantage of the privacy provided by the few hours of darkness. I found my toilet kit, a few strips of toilet paper and the small pack of matches mandated by Wiley. I crawled out of my tent, clicked on my headlamp, and headed toward the yellow-flagged pole next to the bushes.

I quietly walked up the beach. At one point I stopped, thinking that I had heard a strange sound coming from the direction where Kathy and Angie had pitched their tent. The sound was low and long, sounding like an animal in pain. For a moment, I imagined a wolf or a grizzly devouring some unfortunate creature, but the sound vanished and so I thought little more of it.

I took up the shovel, dug a hole, clicked off my headlamp so as not to attract attention. Afterward, I struck the match and lit the edges of the toilet paper as per Wiley's instructions. I shoveled dirt over the smoldering remains of the toilet paper, turned my headlamp back on and headed back out to the beachhead. And then I heard another strange sound, this time a high-pitched moaning. I crouched down alongside the bushes and swept the beam of my headlamp across the beach. In the passing light, I noticed someone sitting on the trunk of a dead tree, elbows on knees, head in hands.

"Kathy?" I whispered. She didn't turn. My lamp threw her shadow across the beach; from the way her shoulders moved it looked like she was crying, yet it didn't seem like the sounds I'd heard were coming from her. I sat down alongside her, the moaning now clearly coming from further down the beach. "Kathy, you okay?" Kathy's face remained hidden within her hands. She shook her head as the moaning grew louder—and then I understood. "Is Butch in there?" Kathy nodded. "That's just fucked-up."

"No, David, it's not fucked up." The beam from my headlamp caught her flush in the face as she turned toward me, her cheeks glimmering with smeared tears. "Turn that damn thing off, please," she hissed. In the darkness, I heard her sigh, blow her nose. "Angie is a grown woman," she said. "She just happens to enjoy—well, you know. Not that I don't, it's just that her opportunities seem to come easier than mine do."

Now there were two sounds, one high and shrill, one rough and low, calling to each other, coming faster and faster and then—nothing. "Maybe we should go see if the tent's still standing," I said.

She punched me in my shoulder.

"Can I ask you a question?" Kathy asked after a while.

"Shoot."

"Promise you won't take it wrong?"

"I've got thicker skin than you think."

"Good. So here's my question. Are you—gay?" I half-smiled and shook my head. "Don't get me wrong, there's nothing wrong with being gay. At least half of my clients are gay. The only problem with being gay is if you try to hide it, because that leads to a lot of repression and unnecessary unhappiness."

"Kathy, I'm not gay."

"You sure?"

"Completely, one hundred percent sure."

"Interesting, but I guess I'm just a little confused."

"Why confused?" I said.

"Because yesterday morning—"

"The water was cold."

"It wasn't that."

"It really was," I said.

"Come on, David."

"All right," I sighed. "I guess not. At least not completely."

"I figured. Then what? I know that some guys don't like this look." She ran her fingers through her short hair.

"For the record, I like your hair. I think you're very attractive."

"Thanks, I guess. So, what is it? Are you gun-shy? Your heart's been broken, you don't want to take any more chances?"

"We're going to be dead tomorrow. We should get some sleep."

"We *are* going to be dead tomorrow, or maybe the next day, or the day after that—isn't that the point?" In the soft, sad way she said it, it seemed as if she were offering her words not specifically to me, but to the vast, dark emptiness surrounding us. "That's it, isn't it?" she said, expressing more sadness than exaltation at her apparent epiphany. "Your heart's been broken."

"You're good at what you do."

"I've had enough practice."

"It's not worth talking about. It happened, big shit."

"But here's the thing, David. I think it's still happening."

"I don't know—"

Kathy grabbed hold of my arm. "Shhh—did you hear that?" Sounds of feet crunching the sandy gravel, coming our way from the camp.

"Probably just somebody who wants to use the bathroom," I whispered.

Whoever it was clicked on a flashlight, pointing straight down at the beach. "Stay low and quiet, maybe he'll miss us," Kathy whispered back. She slipped down off the log and pulled me down with her. I squeezed against her, the two of us sitting low on the damp, stony sand, the log pressing against our spines.

"He may miss us, or he may trip over us," I said.

"*Shhh!*"

"Butch, where the hell are you?" It was Zack, whispering in that gruff way where you might as well not bother to whisper at all. "You dumb shit, if you're where I think you are—" He raised the flashlight and pointed it in the direction of Kathy and Angie's tent.

"Damn, he knows!" she whispered. "I can't let him—"

Before I could stop her, she sprang to her feet, standing squarely in Zack's beam.

"Jesus!" Zack whispered. "You scared the shit out of me!"

"*I* scared the shit out of *you*?" Kathy said.

"Damn straight! You coulda been a fucking bear or something."

"Well I'm not, so relax."

Zack cocked his head. "What are you doin' out here alone in the middle of the night, anyways?"

"Just—getting some night air."

"There's plenty of night air in your tent, unless there's someone else in there sucking all the air out."

"No one's doing any sucking—" Kathy said and then buried her face in her hand.

"My brother's in there, ain't he?" Zack made a move to bypass Kathy, but she stepped in his way. Much as I hated to do it, I figured it was time for me to show myself. "Doc, you're out here too?" He shined his light in my face.

I covered my eyes with my arm and turned away. "In person," I said.

"If Butch is in that tent, I'm gonna drag him out."

"Zack, tell you what. Maybe just leave him alone."

"But he's—"

"I know what he's doing. Forget about it."

"Angie's a big girl," Kathy said.

Zack stared at Kathy. "You mean, it don't matter to you that you're out here while she's in there with him?"

"Not to me," Kathy said. "That's what friends are for."

"If someone pulled that shit in my tent and I had to bail out at two o'clock in the morning, I'd be pretty pissed off," Zack said. "This is bullshit. My dad would cut his nuts off if he found out. He told him clear as day, no more messing around with the women fishermen—fisherwomen—whatever."

"He does this a lot?" Kathy said. For some reason, she sounded surprised.

Zack laughed. "Anytime he gets a chance, which ain't all that often, since we don't get too many ladies coming out here with us. When it does happen, he usually waits 'till the last night we're camping. What's this, only the second night? Bet you a buck he's done with her by the time we're back at Nalunaq."

Kathy nudged me. "Don't even think about taking that bet!" she whispered. "Zack, maybe it's time you just head off to your tent," she said, sounding like an uptight chaperone at an overnight camp for kids. "I'm pretty sure Butch will be coming up for air pretty soon, and when he does, I'll send him back your way."

Zack stood there for a few moments. "Sorry, but I gotta get him," he finally said.

We all went quiet at the sound of the unzipping of the tent flap down the beach. "Probably my douche-bag brother," he said. "About damn time."

"Just please leave him be," Kathy said.

Zack turned toward me. "Doc?"

"I think she's right. Everything's cool, just let it slide."

"Fuckin'-a," Zack said under his breath.

Butch walked toward us. "What the hell you all doin' out here?" he said cheerfully.

"What are *we* doin'?" Zack said. "What the hell are *you* doin'?" Zack sniffed the night air. "Jesus, what's that?"

"I have no fucking idea what you're talking about."

The scent of the incense had saturated Butch's clothes. He reeked of it.

Another tent zipper unzipped, this time from the direction of camp. Zack focused his light beam at the sound. Someone was crawling ass backward out of a tent. He stood up, turned toward the light, and shielded his eyes against it. "Shit, it's Larry," I whispered. He clicked on his headlamp, headed toward the bushes and, with his back turned toward us, urinated into the tangle of leaves and branches. Zack never bothered to lower his light, the beam reflecting off the *EAGLES* insignia imprinted on the backside of his green sweatpants in bold, silver lettering, just above the screaming eagle-head symbols of his beloved football team emblazoning each butt cheek. He wiped his hands on his sweats then headed our way, his hand shielding his eyes from Zack's light.

"What the hell you all doing?" he said.

"Seems to be the question of the night," I said.

He scanned the faces and spotted Kathy. "Damn, why didn't you tell me she was out here? You could've at least let me pee in private."

"Don't worry about it," Kathy said. "We enjoyed the artwork."

"Huh?"

"*Fly, Eagles, fly, on the road to victory!*" Kathy sang.

We heard the sound of another zipper unzipping—Kathy and Angie's tent again. Beams of light now focused upon buttocks draped in neon-pink sweats backing out through the flaps. Angie zipped the panel, shielded her eyes from our lights, and sashayed across the beach. She arrived in her own cloud of sweet-smelling incense, her hair drooping down over one eye. She sidled over to Butch, hung her hands on his shoulder, nuzzled against his neck. "Welcome to the party," I said.

"I'm partied out," she replied. "I just want to pee." She stroked her nose against Butch's scraggly beard. "Want to come with?"

Butch winked at Zack and headed off with Angie toward the shovels. "He pulls that shit around my dad, and I swear to God he'll bust his sorry ass," Zack said.

"All right, I kinda get it now," Larry said. "How about the two of you take our tent?" He nodded to me and Kathy. "And don't anyone ever say that I'm not a great brother."

Before I could respond to Larry's offer, Kathy wrapped her arms around my waist. "Thanks, but it's late and we've got some serious fishing to do tomorrow. *Rain check*?" she said and dug a knuckle into my spine.

"Any time," Larry said. "How about we head back to bed, bro? Babcock says we're getting into silver territory tomorrow."

"Silvers definitely are runnin'," Zack said. "Not sure they're this high up yet, but once we get down the river some, they'll be there."

Another zipper unzipped. Our lights illuminated the face of Carl Cooper protruding from his tent. "Will you all shut the fuck up!" he shouted. "Some of us are trying to get some sleep!" He popped back inside his tent and zipped himself in.

"Pleasant fellow," I said.

"Silver salmon," Larry said. "Damn, I can't wait!"

Kathy brought her mouth close to my ear. "Neither can I," she whispered.

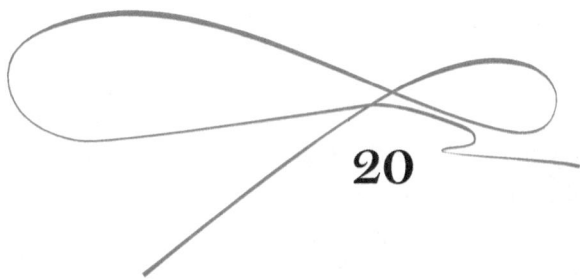

20

It was around now that I lost track of time; the long days and short nights, absent requirements for meetings, lecturing, or conducting lengthy, precisely scheduled experiments, ushering me into a different state of existence, at first unnerving but one which I gradually came to find strangely liberating.

Larry and I ended up in a raft with Wiley, Tommy Ewing, and Rick Garrett. Given the line-up, I figured it would be a quiet day out on the river. Larry generally didn't talk much while he fished, and I had little opportunity or inclination to say anything to Ewing since first meeting him back in Anchorage.

And then there was Rick Garrett. The dour look on his drawn, whisker-stubbled face, the distance he kept from the others, the silence that surrounded him like an impenetrable cloud; he seemed like a guy asking to be left alone, and I was happy to oblige. Unexpectedly, Larry's flies lured him out of his cloud as effectively as they might coax a rainbow trout out of the dark shadows of the cold river into a brilliant leap into air and sun. "That's some beautiful work you've done there," he said to Larry.

"Want to try one?" Larry said. "How about an orange wiggle tail? Babcock says they're great for silvers."

"Yeah?"

"He says rainbows and grayling will hit on them, too."

"Sure you don't mind?" Garrett said. "I'd hate to lose it."

"You kidding? I made a ton of them." For the first time since he tied that nail knot for me when we'd just started out on the river, he set his rod down. He picked up his fly box and slid in alongside Garrett. "Check these out." He poked through the different compartments in the box, explaining the kinds of feathers and beads that he used, how long it took to construct each one, which fish were likely to be attracted to each.

"You musta spent years doin' all this," Garrett said.

"Actually not," Larry said. And then Larry surprised me. Without raising his eyes from the box, Larry told Garrett that he had tied the flies while he was holed up in his hospital room, getting treated for cancer. He hadn't told anyone on the trip about his cancer, except for Wiley, and had made me swear to him that I wouldn't, either. Strange that he would choose to divulge this now, and to Garrett, of all people.

Garrett tied one of Larry's orange wiggle tails to the end of his line and hooked a huge rainbow. With the sun burning through the clouds and warming the river, it wasn't long before everyone was catching more fish than they could have dreamed of. Soon I was sweating beneath my chest waders. I thought about changing out of my heavyweight cotton shirt into something cooler, but this was a pain as it meant digging around in my bag for the one short sleeved T-shirt that I had brought with me. It could wait for our lunch break, I decided, so I pushed up my shirtsleeves and splashed cool river water on my forearms, neck, and head.

Garrett slid the straps of his waders off his shoulders and pulled his army-olive shirt over his head. A nasty burn scar streaked his left arm from his elbow to his shoulder and ran down his left side, webbed patterns from skin grafts shiny in the sun, dense bands of pink scar tissue weaving and swirling around the grafts like thick strokes from the brush of an abstract artist.

"Nasty burn you got there," Larry said. "How'd that happen?"

"Fucking IED," Garrett said. He unbuckled his waterproof bag, unrolled the top and dug his right arm deep inside. "Almost made it out whole. Almost."

"Out of where?" Larry said.

Garrett fished out a black T-shirt, stuffed the long-sleeved shirt he'd been wearing back into the bag, rolled the top up and clicked the buckle closed. "Where? Shit, I was everywhere." He slid his scarred, tightly muscled body into the wrinkled T-shirt, a Dead-head skull in red and blue with a white lightning bolt between the colors staring out from his chest.

"Everywhere?" Larry said.

Garrett nodded. "Started out in Afghanistan. Spent eighteen months in the mountains."

"With the Rangers?" Larry asked. Garrett nodded again. "Tora Bora?"

"Any place you can name, and a shitload of places you ain't never heard of and probably never will," Garrett said. "Then Iraq. Fucking waste—but that's another story. Had about a week and a half left on my deployment. We were heading down to the airport one morning, sweeping the road clear for some hoo-ha coming in from Washington, and then *boom*."

"Boom?" Larry said.

"We missed one. Thought we had 'em figured out; thought we knew what to look for, you know? Guess not," Garrett said through a bitter grin. "But I was lucky. I was sitting in the back, right behind the driver. Fucking thing went off somewhere up front. Lights out for the driver and for a buddy of mine sitting up there next to him. The guy sitting next to me, his neck broke when the Hummer rolled over. He's still in Walter Reed, paralyzed like that Superman actor when he fell off his horse."

"Christopher Reeve," I said.

"Right, Reeve. He's dead now, ain't he?"

"Yeah, a long time ago."

"He'd be better off, too, if you asked me. Can't move nothin' from the neck down. Can't even breathe for himself—hooked up to a machine. I got out with just this burn so I can't complain, I guess." He turned back to Larry. "When I was sitting there in the hospital, waiting for all this to heal up, I shoulda done what you did, use my time more productively. Tying all them flies must have kept you from going bat-shit crazy. I didn't do much except watch TV."

"It wasn't just tying flies that kept me going," Larry said. "I gotta give David some credit, too. He translated what the cancer docs were saying, explaining to me why it made sense for them to run all that poison shit into me. He said that if I didn't get the treatments, I was dead meat. When I first heard about how much chemo I was going to need, and all the side effects, I didn't want it. To me, the drugs sounded worse than the cancer; I figured I might as well do nothing and be done with it. David and my wife talked me into the chemo and then the bone marrow transplant. He can't tie a nail knot worth a damn, but when it comes to that kind of bullshit, I guess he knows what he's talking about." Garrett nodded in my direction. It looked for a moment like he smiled. "Been fishing long?" Larry asked.

"A year or two," Garrett said. "Picked it up from a rehab nurse in Walter Reed. He was big into fly fishing. One day near the end of my rehab, he asked me if I wanted to come out with him. Took me to the Potomac, out past D.C. We fished off a little piece of land on the southeast side of the river. A lot of trees with low branches—tricky for fly casting, especially since I'd never done it before, and my arm was still tight and numb from the burn. Great spot for fishin', though. Caught me a few good-sized striped bass and I never looked back." Garrett whipped his rod above his head and let loose a beautiful, arching cast.

"McDonough's spot—that was the nurse's name, Scott McDonough—his fishing spot was just across the river from Mount Vernon," he said as he worked the fly. "We fished all day, with George Washington's old mansion right up there on the bluff. There was this bald eagle, must've had a nest somewhere around there. She'd glide right down the middle of the river and then back up and then circle way high over the mansion. Seemed like she was looking for something she'd lost somewhere along the way. I was watching that bird and couldn't help thinking what Washington would've thought about Afghanistan and Iraq and all that shit. I kept on with fly fishing, but I never went back there. Couldn't focus." A fish struck Garrett's line. Garrett set the hook and pulled in a small grayling. He gently removed the hook and set the fish back into the river. "Nope, never did go back there," he said, his words punctuated by the whip of his rod slicing the air.

I envied Larry's ability of breaking through walls to reach hard people. In the days when I was seeing patients, I never was much good at it. It served me well to keep some emotional distance between me and them. Some of my friends couldn't keep that kind of separation. After a while, most of them were a mess. If you could do it and keep your sanity, more power to you. But some of us couldn't.

For sure, Larry had a wall, too. The walls around both Larry and Rick Garrett came down for each other that morning.

Larry's recounting of our discussions about his cancer treatments had another effect. Not too long after he told that story to Garrett, I lost a fly; probably snagged on a sunken branch. As I fumbled with a nail knot, struggling to tie a new leader onto my line, Garrett set down his rod and came over to me. "I got that, Doc," he said, and tied the knot for me, tight and firm.

Heavy, gray clouds rolled in after lunch, borne upon a chill wind that made the warm sun of the morning feel like a distant memory. It wasn't long before we were back in our long-sleeved shirts, fleeces, and down vests. The sudden change in the weather seemed to dampen the appetites of the fish; everyone's line hung slack the rest of the afternoon. I could feel the rain coming in the heavy dampness of the wind. I could smell it. I set my rod down, undid my bag, pulled my waterproof jacket up to the top, just in case. Wiley sensed it, too. "Let's hope it holds up until after we set up camp," he said.

As the afternoon wore on, the bracing freshness of the Alaskan air was replaced by a pungent, putrid aroma, the unmistakable stench of death. Rotting carcasses of king salmon, their final spawning completed upon their return after three years in the open sea to this river of their hatching, littered the banks as we silently slid by.

A cold rain had begun to fall by the time we beached the rafts for the night. Wiley, Butch, and Zack cooked up chicken noodle soup and hamburgers, rivulets of rain rolling down their oilskin hats and falling onto the Coleman stoves in sizzling bursts of steam. We ate standing, huddled in our rain gear, trying to the keep our hamburger buns dry. The odor of rotting salmon dulled more than one appetite that evening. For the first time, dinner ended with food left over.

After a while, the rain tapered to a drizzle and then a fine mist. Kathy asked if I'd take a walk with her down the beach. We walked silently for a while among the countless carcasses of rotting salmon. Many of the carcasses were still whole. These were the fresh deaths of late spawners, their once-silver skins mottled with fungus. Kathy stopped alongside a skeleton stripped of its meat except for a bit of muscle and skin left near the tail. "Look at these," she said. She squatted and pointed to tracks that looked like they came from a very large dog. "Wolf," she said. And then I noticed something else, an enormous print that had wiped out more than a few of the wolf prints.

"This one's from a bear," I said.

Up the beach just a bit lay a blue pile amidst the grays of sand and rock. "Bear scat," I said. Kathy nudged a stone through it with the toe of her boot, exposing whole, undigested blueberries within the blue muck. "Looks fresh," I said. "Not sure I'd set up your tent too far outside camp."

"Too late for that, but once I'm inside, I'm not coming out."

"Angie can live with that?"

"Tonight, she has no choice."

Kathy's eyes returned to the river as we walked on. We hadn't gone far when she stopped and squeezed my hand. "Look," she said, and pointed to the shallows.

Countless salmon hovered in the river, heads into the gentle current, tail fins beating to keep themselves in place. Below each fish lay small depressions in the sandy river bottom, each filled with eggs. The pectoral and pelvic fins of the fish fanned the nests with the last bits of energy left to them; their normally sleek, muscular bodies now wasting on the bone; their normally bright, silvery skin now colorless but for white patches of fungus, consuming them while alive. We watched them for what seemed to be a long while, the world around us quiet but for an occasional stray voice from camp, the rustle of leaves in a passing chill breeze, the song of falling water rolling over some nearby rock. Kathy squeezed my hand and lifted it to her face. My skin brushed against her cheek, wiping away a still-warm tear.

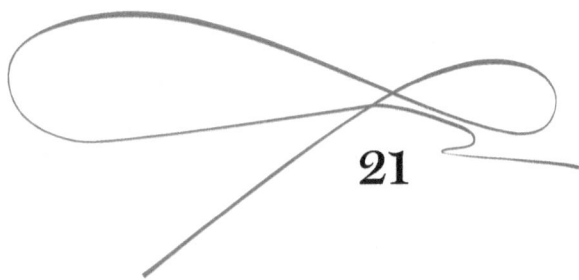

21

The rain began again soon after I climbed into my tent. Although Larry already was asleep, it was not his snoring that kept me awake but the image of the salmon, their instinctive devotion to their nests, unwavering even as time and genetics conspired to make this last heroic endeavor unimaginably difficult. I understood Kathy's tears even as I mourned my nearly lifelong inability to shed a tear of my own.

The rain fell steadily until I faded off to sleep. It had grown heavier by the time I awakened. Gusts of cold wind shook the tent, my breath steaming out from within the warm cocoon of my down sleeping bag. I dreaded the thought of emerging, but Wiley's shrill whistle signaled that I had little choice.

I pulled on nearly every piece of clothing that I'd brought with me: expedition-weight long underwear, jeans beneath my waders, T-shirt, turtleneck, fleece, down vest, waterproof winter ski jacket beneath my fishing vest, three pairs of heavy woolen socks, woolen cap pulled down over my ears, finger-less woolen gloves. Even so, my hands shook so hard with the cold that I struggled to bring spoons of steaming oatmeal to my mouth at breakfast.

I gave up on any idea of fishing that day and imagined that the others would do the same. The whipping of fly rods that began as soon as we pushed off proved my naivete. I sat with my head bowed, the drawstrings of my waterproof hood pulled tight against the stinging rain, my mouth and nose hidden just beneath the top of the high-standing collar of my ski jacket. Larry and the others fished as if it was just another bright, sunny day. Even factoring out the rain, it didn't make sense to me, as I had been told that cold and clouds make for lousy fishing.

Zack was back at the oars. I edged forward in my seat and asked him about this. "You'd be right if we was talkin' about rainbows and Dollys," Zack said. "But we're in silver country now. Silver salmon don't give a shit about the weather. They've swum all the way back here to lay their eggs before they die, and after all that swimmin' they're pretty damn hungry. Rain and wind's not gonna keep 'em from strikin', promise you that." Zack pulled on one oar, steering us away from an island. "You oughta get your rod workin'," he said. "First one to catch a silver gets a prize."

"Prize? What kind of prize?"

"I dunno, just made it up. Just tryin' to get you fishin' after all the money you paid."

"I appreciate it," I said as I tried to suppress the shivers passing through me in time to the waves of rain pelting us. "But I'm good the way I am."

"Maybe you'll feel different when we get to our next stop. It's the best fishin' hole for silvers on the whole river."

"Can't wait," I murmured into the wet collar covering my mouth.

Babcock was the first to latch onto a silver. I heard his shout and watched through the rain as the fish bent his rod down until its tip grazed the water. He stood up, jerking the rod back and forth through wind and rain. After ten minutes of fight, he reached over the side and pulled in his prize. It was a monster of a fish compared to what we'd been catching until then, reaching from Babcock's chest down past his ample belly to his knees as he held it up for a picture. "Twenty pounder, at least," Zack said as he eyed the catch through the rain and swirls of fog hovering over the river. "And you see the way its sides are all bulging out? Eggs. Babcock knows, he'll get her back in the water quick. Hate to hurt her when she's come all this way to lay her eggs, y'know?"

As if on cue, Babcock bent over the side of the raft and set the fish gently into the water. "I hope the others do the same," I said.

"They better or my dad'll kick their damn fool asses."

Butch looked to have found a seam of migrating silvers, as both Kathy's and Tony's rods bent simultaneously under the force of fresh strikes. "Over there!" Larry called out to Zack. "Quick!" Zack rolled his eyes and tugged on his right oar, sending us back toward the middle of the stream. Rick Garrett, riding with us once again, was the first in our raft to hook one. His wasn't the size of Babcock's, and looked different, with a sharply beaked snout and a lot of red on its back, its silver coloring reduced to some thin stripes running down its sides. "That there's a male, and an old one," Zack said. He handed Garrett a pair of pliers to twist the hook from out of the fish's mouth without getting too close to its sharp teeth. "Sucker's too old to eat. Flesh'd taste like cardboard."

Half an hour later, we beached the rafts in an inlet carved out of the left bank. Wiley motioned for us to gather round. "This here's the best spot for silver fishin' on the entire river," he said. "Y'all got one hour, then we gotta get goin'. Whatever you do, do not, and I mean DO NOT go wading into the river. There's a steep drop-off about four feet out, and it's real slick. It gets deep fast. If you take a bath today, it may be your last. Got it?"

I took hold of my woolen hat with sodden, fingerless gloves and slid it low on my forehead to cover any remaining exposed skin. The wind funneled sheets of rain up the river, the waves of flying droplets sounding as if someone was hurling handfuls of small stones against my jacket and waders. An hour before, the thermometer dangling from my fishing vest registered thirty-eight degrees. It felt colder now, the drenching wind cutting through every layer of my clothes down to my shivering skin.

"The first breath of Alaskan winter." This from Wiley, appearing silently and without warning alongside me. Rain dripped from the wide brim of his hat and his rough, red beard.

"This totally sucks," Zack said. "Sometimes we hit some nasty weather beginning right around now, but at least it keeps down the mosquitoes. This?" He opened his gloved hands palm-upwards to the sky, momentarily staring straight into the wind and rain. "I can't remember anything this bad."

A gust of cold, wet wind again cut through my clothes. Butch cursed the sky with his eyes. He headed up toward the scrub with Angie at his side, the two of them disappearing behind the leeward side of a boulder. Wiley, Zack, and I huddled together, our backs turned toward the storm. We were surrounded, suffocated by wind and water. I began to wonder if it was possible to drown standing up. Suddenly, a ray of hope from Zack. "How about we make camp early tonight?" he said to his father.

A dry tent, a warm, dry sleeping bag, an opportunity to

climb out of my sopping wet clothes and kick off my muddy, cold boots. The thought of it spread a wave of warmth through my body like a shot of brandy. The sensation proved false and short-lived.

"Good luck gettin' those folks into camp early," Wiley said. He nodded toward the fishermen along the riverbank. They stood ghostlike, enshrouded within gray veils of rain and wind-blown river fog, silent but for the sounds of rain and river and the rhythmic whip-song of invisible fishing lines.

The stillness of the backwater soon turned to froth as the starved silver salmon struck at the fanciful flies falling upon them like manna. The fishermen danced a kind of Maypole dance along the riverbank, one passing above or below raised or lowered fly rods as they tried to avoid tangling lines. The mud on the riverbank soon became as slippery as soap on wet glass under their boots. Some fell backward as their feet flew out from under them; some flopped forward, landing belly-first in the mud, hands still grasping rods at risk of disappearing into the river under the pull of starved salmon struggling to escape the hooks.

I watched it all with a sadistic sense of hopefulness, figuring that this chaos surely would convince them to bring an early end to the cold misery of this day—until Babcock's booming voice destroyed my dreams. "Wiley, lemme tell you buddy, it don't get no better'n this!" he shouted as he hauled out a silver nearly as large as the one he had caught a while before.

"Tell you what," Wiley said. "Since we're going to be hanging around a little longer, how about I fire up one of the Colemans and warm us up some tomato soup?"

"He must like you," Zack said as Wiley trudged off to the

raft where the stove was stowed. "He just about never gets a Coleman going except at dinner."

"He's probably just as cold as we are," I said. I glanced back at the fishermen and noticed Kathy standing alone, her rod held limply in her hand, her head hanging down. "I'll be right back," I said.

I hurried out toward her and saw she was sobbing. I put my arm around her shoulders. She tensed up, then melted against me. I pulled her closer. "What's wrong?" I asked.

"Look, David. Just look."

Mud-covered fishermen, their eyes wild with excitement, hauled their fat-bellied, silver-skinned trophies from the churning water. They pinned their prizes in the mud, dodged the thrashing tails, and attacked them with open pliers, twisting the hooks from gaping, bleeding mouths, holding their writhing trophies up for the others to see before throwing them back into the water. "Pretty crazy," I said.

"Crazy? It's way worse than crazy. It's *sick*! Those fish are full of eggs. They've come all this way to spawn, and we're torturing them!"

"It's catch and release."

"You don't get it, do you?"

"Why are you pissed at me? I'm not even fishing."

She took a deep, sobbing breath. "You're not, are you?" I imagined a small smile of relief at this, although her face, still turned toward the river, remained cloaked from my view by her hood. "I'm sorry, I'm cold. Wet and cold."

"Come with me. Wiley's firing up the Coleman. Some hot tomato soup will do you good."

We walked hand in hand behind the fishermen, mindful

of the flying lines whipping above our heads. Wiley had set up the stove upwind of the big boulder protecting Butch and Angie. A pot of soup steamed on one of the burners, Zack warmed his hands over the other flame. Butch emerged from behind the boulder and headed toward us. "Smells good," Butch said. He nodded toward the fishermen. "Just look at those crazy fuckers."

"One thing I've been meaning to ask," I said. "How did you all learn about the ledge in the river? The one you warned us about."

Wiley, Zack, and Butch looked at each other, waiting for someone to answer. "One of our clients, an asshole lawyer from L.A., waded out and slipped off it on one of our first trips," Wiley finally said.

"The river was pretty new to us then," Butch added.

"I know, you used to run the Salmon River," I said. Wiley looked at me, surprised. "The pilot told me on the way out," I explained.

"I hope he didn't tell you no more than that," Wiley said.

"Nope, I made sure of that," Zack said. "Secret River, that's all I'd let him say."

"That's the name of this river we're on?" Kathy said. "The Secret River?"

"That's what they're calling it," I said.

"And that's what we're gonna keep callin' it," Wiley said. "Make sure I get around to havin' a talk with Luke when we get back," he said to Zack. "Gotta remind him to keep his mouth shut."

"Anyways, you're right, we used to run the Salmon River," Butch said. "Only after a while, it seemed like everybody was fishin' the Salmon. Left all kinds of crap all over the riverbanks—cans and broken bottles, charred wood from their fires, toilet paper from where the bears dug it up—shit like that."

"Didn't hardly feel like wilderness anymore," Wiley said.

"Me and Butch, we was right there," Zack said. "We saw him go under—"

"You shoulda seen the look on his face," Butch said. "Eyeballs poppin' out of his skull. Kinda like the river was some big ole' snake swallowing him up feet first."

"What did you do?" Kathy said.

"I tell you what we shoulda done," Butch said. "We shoulda let the asshole drown."

"Right, and let Dad get sued," Zack said. "We pulled him out, that's what we did. Butch and me, we got hold of him when he came up for air and just pulled that sucker straight out. Son of a bitch moaned and groaned about it the rest of the trip. That's why we call this the Moan and Groan hole."

"The Moan and Groan hole?" I said.

"Yeah," Zack said. "That was my idea. Has a nice ring to it, don't you think? Maybe I really am a poet," he said and smiled.

"Soup's ready," Wiley said. He poured it out, steaming in the river-washed bowls we'd used for our breakfast oatmeal. We drank it straight from our bowls, the smell of it delicious, the soup warming us from the inside out.

I wiped the corners of my mouth with the pad of my thumb and licked it clean. "Does it happen a lot, people falling into the river like that?"

"Not since I started warning them," Wiley said. "But, you know, on most every trip, you get somebody who's got that potential."

We sipped our soup, watching the fisherman through the rain and fog, listening to the rods as they sliced through the wet, heavy air. "So, Doc," Butch said after a while, "what is it that you do again?"

"He's a research doc, not a real doc—ain't that right?" Zack said.

"Actually, I did have clinical training—"

"It's all got something to do with cells dyin'," Zack said. He stroked the water from his golden beard, appearing deep in thought. "But here's what I don't get. Why are you spendin' all that time in a laboratory doin' research on how shit dies? Ain't you supposed to be out there keepin' people alive?"

I was thinking about an answer when I heard a shout.

Zack and Butch were running full-out, Wiley right behind, before I could get a sense of what was going on. "C'mon!" Kathy said.

I took off after Kathy and Wiley, running across the muddy beach as quickly as I could. The fishermen had gathered at the edge of the water, their rods scattered in the mud. Butch and Zack pushed their way through to the front, the fishermen closing ranks behind them. Babcock's big body made up most of the back of the scrum. I tugged on his shoulder. "What the hell's going on?"

"Somebody fell in!"

"Who?"

"Can't tell."

"It's Russ!" Bob Billings called out in a panic. "For Christ's sake, Russ is in the fucking river!"

Russ? Shit, cold water can stop anyone from breathing. When you have lung disease as bad as Russ's—"Let me through!" I shouted. I squeezed between Babcock and Tony, up to the river's edge. Wiley, Butch, and Zack stood in a human chain, Wiley's feet planted heels-first in the mud, his right arm reaching out, his hand grasping Butch's who held onto Zack, standing waist-deep in the river, his hand clamped around Russ's wrist. Russ floundered in the water, submerged but for his head, his hand clutching onto Zack. His breaths came in gasps, his face blue as ice, his eyes wide, white, desperate.

With teeth bared through his dripping beard, Zack tugged Russ out to his shoulders, then took hold of the collar of his waterlogged coat. Larry and Garrett splashed past and grabbed onto Russ's arms. Together, they hauled Russ coughing and gasping from the river.

Russ fought for breath, sounding as if someone had him around the throat. He retched and vomited up his breakfast. I knelt alongside him, he was shaking badly in his cold, wet clothes. "We're going to sit you up," I said. He raised a trembling hand, asking for time to get his breath. Larry and Garrett lifted him to sitting. "We've got to get you out of these and dry you off," I said.

"I'll get a towel," Kathy said.

"We got a thermal blanket in the emergency kit," Wiley said. "Bring that, too."

Larry and I pulled off his jacket and vest and slid his arms out of the suspenders to his waders. We lifted him up and peeled off the waders, a few gallons of icy river water spilling from inside his pants. A moment later, Russ stood naked, blue, and shivering on the beach, his hands cupped over his genitals. Kathy came jogging back, the towel and insulated silvery blanket clutched against her chest. She handed me the towel. I dried Russ off as best I could in the windblown waves of rain and took the blanket from Kathy. "Here, put this around you," I said. "Now we need to find you some dry clothes."

Larry and I guided Russ to the boulder. Angie saw us coming and vacated her protected spot. We stood him up there at least partially shielded from the windblown rain. Somebody handed me his bag; I fished out some dry clothes and helped him get dressed. Just stepping into his pants set him breathing hard through tightly pursed lips. By the time we had layered on his dry clothes, he was gulping in air through a wide-open mouth and wheezing it back out. I suggested to Wiley that we get going and make camp early, as Zack had suggested earlier.

Butch and Zack broke down the stove and stowed it inside one of the rafts. I kept a close eye on Russ as he huddled behind the boulder. His breathing seemed to be getting worse; I dropped down onto a knee alongside of him. "Hey Russ, you all right?" He nodded. "Russ, you've got to talk to me, okay?" A thought tightened my stomach. "You having chest pain?" He answered with silence. "The angina from a long time ago, is it back?"

Russ's eyes seemed to grow wider, his breathing faster than before. I thought I detected a subtle nod. "Close your eyes, take some deep, easy breaths," I said. "I'll be right back."

I sprang to my feet and rummaged through Russ's bag until I found the bottle of nitroglycerin pills. "You need to put this under your tongue, let it dissolve," I said. Russ nodded, opened his mouth. I dropped a pill beneath his tongue. "You feeling a tingle?" He nodded again and closed his eyes.

Wiley came over with Zack and Butch alongside. "What's going on?" Wiley said.

"He's got some chest pain," I said.

"You tellin' me he's havin' a heart attack?"

"I hope not, let's see what the pill does. We need to hang here for another ten or fifteen minutes, maybe give him another one and see how he feels."

"You gave him one of them pills those assholes almost made us leave back in Anchorage?" Zack said.

"You got it."

"Damn lucky we brought 'em."

"Looks like it," I said.

"Tell you what. If I ever see that son-of-a-bitch T.J. and those hunters again, I'm going to kick the living shit out of 'em," Zack said.

"Not if I get to 'em first," Butch said. I glanced at Wiley and sensed that he was feeling the same way.

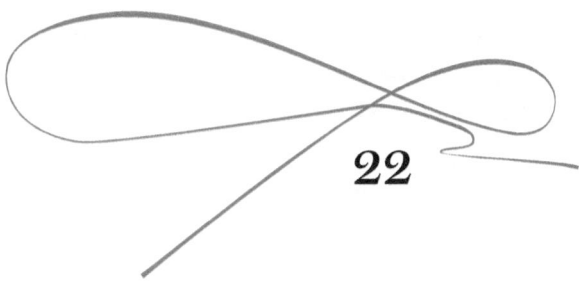

22

We made camp early on another rock-strewn beach some-where along the Secret River. The river was wider here. You could see the effect of the heavy rain, the water now rough and wild, branches both long dead and freshly fallen sweeping by in the dark, angry water. Dead king salmon lined the banks, layered two to three deep in those places where the highest reach of the current had deposited them, the air around them pocketed with invisible clouds smelling of rotting fish flesh.

The rain ended sometime toward the end of dinner, leaving a chilly evening, a feel of mid-autumn in the air. Larry joined Babcock and a few of the others for some post-dinner fishing, anxious to compensate for opportunities they missed as we sped downstream with the current, passing by a number of other fishing holes to get Russ settled in his tent.

I finished my dinner, headed back to my tent, removed my boots and coat, and dove into my sleeping bag, delighting in the all-encompassing warmth. I thought about reading but instead closed my eyes and settled deeper into the goose-down heaven that surrounded me.

And then I heard footsteps approaching; Larry returning for an extra layer of clothes, I figured. The footsteps stopped outside the entrance, a long, quiet hesitation. Definitely not Larry. I buried myself deeper in my bag, hoping that the intruder would go away.

"Mind if I have a look-see at your digs?" Kathy said from outside.

I yawned, wiped my eyes. "If you want," I said.

Kathy unzipped the tent flap and poked her head inside. "Spare but livable."

"No incense."

"That's Angie's doing, not mine."

"And she is—?"

"Currently occupied? Yeah, I guess."

"Already? It's not even dark yet."

"David, why would you even think that matters?"

Kathy kicked off her camp shoes, crawled inside, zipped up the screen flap. She sat down on the far end of Larry's sleeping bag, folding her legs up beneath her. "Nice bag," she said. "Bet it keeps your brother snug and warm."

"He sleeps like a baby, except for the snoring."

"Must be nice, sleeping like a baby."

"You're not a good sleeper?"

"Not really."

"Ever get checked for sleep apnea?" I said.

"Oh, please." She cocked her head as if mulling something over, then leaned toward me, her hands on her knees, elbows bowed out. "I just stopped by to tell you that you did a nice job back there with Russ."

"Zack, Butch, and Wiley fished him out, with some help from Larry and Garrett. Not me."

"But you saved him from a heart attack."

"And you saved him from hypothermia by bringing over

that blanket."

"Not exactly the same," she said.

"I just put a pill under his tongue."

"You don't give yourself enough credit," she said. "Maybe Zack had a point when he said that doctors like you were supposed to spend their time keeping people alive, not studying how cells die."

"That's pretty simplistic. My research is relevant to clinical medicine, just farther upstream."

"Can we please skip the river metaphors?"

"Under the circumstances, absolutely."

"Thanks. I'm just saying that it's too bad you don't take care of patients. You have a good bedside manner."

"I don't know. I think I'm better with cells."

"Because you don't need to talk to them?"

"There is that."

She leaned toward me. "So, I've got a theory. You want to hear it?"

"Do I have a choice?"

"Not really, no." Kathy unknotted her feet. She stretched out on Larry's bag, lying flat on her stomach, her chin propped in hands, her face six inches from mine. "So, here's my theory. Deep down, you're afraid of death."

I thought about it for a second. "Is that unusual?"

"No—I mean you're *really* afraid. Like to the point where it rules your life."

"Where are you getting this from?"

"Not sure," she said. "Maybe it's the way you look when we see all those dead fish."

"They stink."

"I think it's more than that."

"They really do stink. Something awful."

"Okay, so they stink." She knocked her heels together a few times. "But I think I'm right about it. I think that's why you do what you do."

"What do I do?"

"Your research. You study dying cells. You want to control death. You control something, you don't fear it anymore."

I rolled my eyes. "If you can understand how cells die, you also might learn about how cells don't die; why cells don't die when they should die."

"Like in cancer?"

"Exactly. If you understand that, maybe you can do something about it."

She ran her hands through her hair, her fingers leaving tracks. Her hair looked good unwashed. She settled her chin back in her hands, her expression now different. "Okay," she said. "Can I ask you a question?"

"Anything. Can't promise I'll answer."

"No, it can't work that way. You need to answer." She sighed. "Okay, I'll tell you what. You answer my question, or questions, and you get to do the same to me."

"Ask you questions?"

"Yup."

"And you'll answer?"

"Yup."

"I show you mine and you show me yours?"

"Something like that. Higher stakes, especially since you've already had a free look."

"Unintended. I really was just out to pee." I lay back down and folded my hands behind my head. I heard a distant shout from one of the fishermen. Somebody caught something they were happy with. "All right," I said. "Go for it."

"Question number one. Your mother—"

"Oh, shit."

"You promised."

I had, but already regretted it. "She died when I was eleven," I blurted out. "Nothing else to say."

"I'm sorry to hear it," Kathy said. "Did your dad ever remarry?"

"Is that question number two?"

"One-B."

"No. Never."

"Okay. Here's one-C. What did she die from, if you don't mind me asking."

I bolted up to sitting, resting on my elbows. I think I startled her. "Poorly differentiated adenocarcinoma, probably ovarian in origin," I said, sounding as cold and dispassionate as if I were reading the diagnosis from my mother's hospital death note. "By the time it was diagnosed, it already was metastatic to her spine, liver, lungs, and brain. It was the brain mets that got her. Mercifully," I added.

"Mercifully?"

"She couldn't breathe on account of the pleural effusions. She couldn't walk with the mets to her spine. She couldn't take any more radiation. In that situation, brain mets are a blessing. They expand, you die. Quickly. Quietly. Peacefully."

Her expression changed. "That's a lot for an eleven-year-old to know about how his mother died."

"Yes, it is." I rolled onto my side, resting my head on one arm. "Except I didn't know any of it when I was eleven. I checked her records later. About twenty-five years after she died, her oncologist at Penn invited me to give a talk there.

He was an old guy already. Before coming, for some reason I asked if he could get hold of a copy of her chart."

"You learn anything? From the records?"

"Like I said, I learned why she couldn't breathe. I learned why her back hurt so bad all the time, although I'd already guessed that when I learned about bone mets during a biology course in high school. We always thought that she had ovarian cancer—"

"She didn't?"

"The cancer was highly undifferentiated. *Possibly* ovarian in origin. Couldn't tell for sure back then. Now we probably could with the tissue markers we have, but that's water under the bridge."

"Again with the water?"

"Sorry. Anyway, my dad died thinking that ovarian cancer killed her, and that's what my brother thinks, and, you know, they very well may be right, so that's the way it's going to stay."

"And your dad?"

"What about my dad? He's dead, too."

Kathy lowered her eyes. "How?"

"Is this question two?"

"Sure, question two."

"Heart attack. Boring, I guess."

"I don't think of a heart attack as boring. Why boring?"

"Not a whole lot to it. His secretary came into his office, found him face-down on his desk. Larry said he was dead long before the EMTs arrived. Technically, he probably died from a terminal arrhythmia. His heart's beating all right one second, then a misfire and that's it. Not the worst way to go, I guess. Painless, quick, no time to think about it.

Hospitals, hospice, pain, dementia, wasting away—all that horror skipped."

"No time to say good-bye, either."

"There is that. Poetic justice I guess, him dying at his desk."

"He was a workaholic?"

"He worked hard. But he also made time for fishing, an occasional round of golf."

"With your brother."

"When Larry got old enough. He mostly went with friends."

"But not with you."

"This must be question twelve already. When do I get the floor?"

Kathy smiled. "You'll get your chance." She shifted, reached out with one hand, tapped the tip of her pointer finger against my own as it lay motionless atop the nylon of the sleeping bag, the clicking of her nail on mine approximating the beating of my heart, somehow sensing the rhythm, even as I sensed her heart beating in lockstep with mine, a strange, unexplainable synchronization. "Okay, you ready for another?" she said.

"I'm not going anywhere."

"Good. So, for this next question, I want you to answer with the first thing that comes to your mind."

"The first thing."

"That's right, the first thing. Don't even think about it. Just blurt it out."

"I'm not a blurter," I said, "at least not usually."

Kathy looked me straight in the eyes. "Tell me about—her."

"Her?"

"The heartbreaker."

I sighed, dropped my head. When I again looked at her, her eyes were still fixed on me. "Not much to say. I met her.

I fell in love with her, whatever the hell that means. It didn't work out. *Voila*, that's it."

"What's her name?"

"Emma."

"Where'd you meet?"

"College. During my senior year. She was a sophomore. We met in a Shakespeare class. We had some laughs over our God-awful professor. He tried to turn Romeo and Juliet into light porn."

"It may have been, in its time," Kathy said. "But this is what I don't get. If you, young, reasonably good-looking—"

"Reasonably?"

"I don't need you getting a swelled head. Anyway, how is it that a young, *reasonably* good looking, good person as far as I can tell, and with a future as a doctor, decides to love someone, and that person doesn't love you back?"

"I don't know. Maybe I'm not all that lovable."

"I doubt that's the problem. There must have been a reason. Somebody else? Quarterback of the football team?"

"No, no quarterback. She just didn't want a relationship. Too early. Too constraining."

"What did she end up doing?"

"Became a photojournalist, infatuated with Sebastião Salgado."

"Salgado. Didn't he take the famous shot of that gold mine somewhere in South America? The workers climbing up and down the ladders into that huge pit—"

"And the shots of the oil workers capping the blown wellheads in Kuwait after the war."

"He took those, too?"

"Definitely."

"Quite a role model. Your friend Emma sets her sights high."

"She shot a story for *The New Yorker* last year on refugee camps in South Sudan. Won a bunch of prizes. Nominated for a Pulitzer."

"A Pulitzer? Amazing!"

"She didn't win, but it was impressive just to be considered. Last I heard, she's working on a piece about miner's rights in South Africa. She's been down there for almost a year."

"Wow. Sounds like she *really* didn't want to be constrained. Do you still keep in touch?"

"Not really. Mostly through mutual friends."

"Doesn't sound like she's a relationship person. You shouldn't take that personally."

"I don't. More power to her."

"Amen."

"So, is that the end of your questions?"

"The prosecution rests. Call the next witness to the stand."

"Finally. All right, do you, Kathy—"

"You don't remember my last name."

"You didn't remember mine. Anyway, I don't even think you ever told me."

"For the record, your honor, it's Sands."

"Okay, so do you, Kathy Sands, swear to tell the truth the whole truth and nothing but the truth, so help you God?"

"What if I don't believe in God?"

"Maybe pretend you do, just this once."

"You're asking a lot, but I'll try."

"All right then, do you swear?"

"Maybe."

"Not good enough."

"Okay, yes. I swear."

"Why are you here?"

"That's your question?"

"Yeah."

"Sorry, but I need more clarity. Here, like on this fishing trip? Here, like in this tent with you? Here, like walking the face of the earth?"

"The middle one."

She rolled onto her back, her arms spread wide. "Maybe I was just a little lonely. Maybe I was looking for someone to talk to while..."

"While your roomie was otherwise occupied?"

"I guess."

"I'm going to guess it's a little bit more than that. At least I hope it is." I reached out, touched the tips of her fingers with mine.

"You think? How could you tell?"

"I had a sense that first time you looked at me, right after we got off the plane. The way you stared out from under that Yankees cap."

"It was that obvious?"

"I'm still trying to get my head around all of this."

"Stop trying so hard," Kathy said. She slid closer to me, took my hand in hers. "Go with the flow. See where it takes you—takes us."

It had grown darker. Larry and the others would be back soon. I felt like I was suffocating. I wished that the rain fly was off the tent, that a breeze could flow in through the screens, allowing me once again to breathe. "We only met a few days ago," I said.

"It's been five days since you got off that plane and found

out about the missing luggage. Five days since I helped you clean up the dinner from our hotel's four-star living quarters."

"Not exactly a romantic introduction," I said.

"Not exactly, no."

I heard footsteps outside. I thought it might be Larry returning. Whoever it was passed us by. "I have another question. I'm just not sure I want to ask it."

"I told you, anything's fair game," she said.

"All right. I can't stop thinking about your father and your brother. You mentioned that they worked at Cantor Fitzgerald. Were they there when...?"

She pulled her hand back. For a moment, it sounded as if she'd stopped breathing. "Yeah, they were there." She sighed. "Not much to talk about, really; everyone knows what happened. I was in my office downtown. Beautiful September day, blue sky, you know the story. Suddenly, the day wasn't so beautiful. Suddenly, the day turned really, really ugly." She rolled toward me, her face looking very different than before, her brows lowered over narrowed eyes. "But if you're looking for some kind of gut-wrenching description of the last desperate minutes of my father and my—my brother—you're not going to get it here. As far as I'm concerned, the plane crashed into the tower and exploded and that was that. They never knew what hit them."

"I'm sorry," I said. I reached out and clasped her hand.

More footsteps outside, voices, laughter. Kathy sat up. "I probably should scoot before we get people talking."

"Let them talk. There's nothing to talk about."

"No, there's not," Kathy said. She smiled sadly. "Mind if I ask one more question?"

"Seriously?"

"Just a simple one. What's going to happen to Russ? Can he still be out there fishing?"

"Well, I doubt he actually had a heart attack; I think he got the nitro in time to prevent that. I guess he can keep fishing, as long as he doesn't fall in again. Besides, you think anyone could stop him? That would really give him a heart attack."

"Makes sense, I guess. You think we could ride together tomorrow?"

"Sure, I'd like that. You can bring Angie, too."

"You're sweet." She kissed my cheek. "I better go before we're busted." She crawled to the entrance flap and unzipped the screen.

"Come on back if your tent is still crowded."

"You, me, and Larry? Now that would be cozy."

I sat up, zipped the screen. Listening to Kathy's quick steps heading out into the night. Sensing there was something more to her story, something she wasn't telling me. Sensing there was something else as strongly as I sensed her heart beating in time with mine just a few moments before. Realizing that there is so much I don't understand, will never understand. Difficult for a scientist like me to acknowledge. Humbling. I crawled back into my sleeping bag and closed my eyes, taking unexpected comfort in the idea of insolvable mysteries.

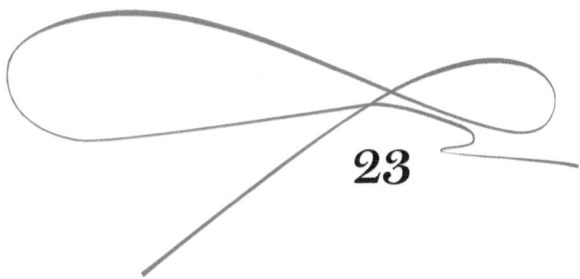

23

Wiley awakened us early, hoping to make up distance lost when we stopped short of his usual camping spot because of Russ and the weather. We ate quickly in the pre-dawn gray; cold cereal, no time to cook the oatmeal, bacon, and scrambled eggs that had kept us going through long mornings of fishing. He lit only one burner, fire for our coffee; pre-emptive defense against a potential mutiny.

We walked the beach, our breath steaming in the morning chill as the first golden rays of the rising sun crept above the nearby eastern hills. The clouds had departed at some point in the night leaving a royal blue sky. Kathy left Angie to fend for herself in Butch's raft and joined us. Larry and Rick Garrett took the prime fishing seats in the back corners of the raft, leaving Kathy and me alone in the bow. It was an ideal arrangement. There was more room up front, a wooden plank spanning the width of the raft serving as our seat, an opportunity to stretch my legs a bit and watch the diamond sparkles of morning sun light up the river as the densely forested hills slid by on either side, the cottonwoods and birches cloaked in lavish, late-summer green, here and there dappled with splashes of yellow and orange, telltales of a looming autumn. It was quiet but for the *whip-whip-whip* of Larry's and Rick Garrett's rods slicing the air, a holy silence in a grand, green, and sapphire sepulcher. Even Wiley seemed reluctant to disturb the tranquil beauty surrounding us, refraining from breaking the still surface of the river with his oars, allowing the current to silently slide us downriver.

I chose to leave my rod at my side that morning, more than content to sit and watch and listen, notebook and pen in hand, jotting down impressions as the spirit moved me. Kathy fished halfheartedly, spending long moments between infrequent casts to glance at me, smiling self-consciously as I returned her smile. At some point, she put her rod down and slid close to me, her shoulder resting on mine.

The sun climbed higher, rising fully above the surrounding hilltops. In the distance lay a broad bend in the northward flow, taking us east. Our raft led the others downstream. Sitting in the bow, I witnessed the river unspoiled, a winding ribbon of green snaking around a sun-glimmering bend. Wiley touched his right oar to the surface, the curved edge sending out a tiny wake as it turned us into the heart of the current.

We glided around the bend, the low sun now beaming straight into our faces. Even with my sunglasses on, it was difficult to see. I shielded my eyes with my hand, squinted and lowered my gaze against the glare. As I awaited the blinding streak of sunglow to fade from my eyes, Kathy's fingers dug into my thigh. "*Ohhh!*" she said, an exhortation as reverent as it was excited. Her arm reached out, finger pointing downstream.

I squinted through the glare, then I saw him.

A bear stood on a logjam atop a point of land jutting out

from the left bank into the stream. It was a grizzly, larger than any bear I could have imagined. Water dripped from the auburn fur on his immense front paws as he reared up on his hind legs, gazing up the river, seemingly straight at us.

Wiley saw him as well. He gestured for Larry and Garrett to stop fishing. He signaled for quiet with a finger to his lips and gently docked the oars. "We're upwind of him," Wiley said in his softest whisper. "Current's takin' us right for him. We might get in pretty close if we stay still and quiet."

We rode the current. Behind us, the other rafts hadn't yet made it around the bend. The bear loomed larger as we drifted closer, awesome and beautiful and terrible, the sound of his breathing coming to us in puffs steaming from his nostrils and half-opened, big-toothed mouth. His wild scent hung in the cool morning air, setting my heart pounding, my skin tingling in a primitive, instinctual response. Something moved at its feet—a freshly caught salmon, its silver skin flashing as it arched its back, tail upward-pointing, mouth wide and gills flaring in the killing air.

We drew closer still. Now he seemed to sense us, his black-tipped snout raised, sniffing. He raised himself higher, eclipsing the sun, the wet, up-sticking fur about his massive head, arms, and shoulders filtering the light into a scintillating corona of rainbows.

We were borne relentlessly forward by the river, the changing angle of our eyes relative to the bear dampening the spectral glow as quickly as it had appeared. We drifted still closer. He had our scent now. He stared straight at us with eyes too small for his head and most assuredly saw us. He shook his head as if in disbelief of our recklessness, our arrogance in light of our laughable insignificance, then opened his mouth wide and with steaming breath sent forth an agonized bellow, a resonant note of ursine outrage. Kathy wrapped her arms around me as the bear dropped to all fours, rocking the logjam with the force of his weight, sending a wave out across the river, rocking our raft. His head dropped low between his mighty shoulders, mouth opened fierce and wide. I glanced around the raft for the shotgun but didn't see it. Just as I feared his impending charge, he clamped his jaw through the back of the frantically flapping fish at his feet. Once more, he raised himself high up upon his rear legs, fish-blood streaming from the doomed salmon onto his matted fur, then twisted and lunged from the logjam, crashing through the underbrush and disappearing into the forest.

We drifted on in silence, Larry and Garrett too stunned to pick up their rods, the oars at Wiley's side all but forgotten. Kathy's arms remained wrapped around my chest, the tremors in her body shaking me. I pulled her closer, noticed faint traces of perfume and sweat, the scent of her breath. It had been there before, all of it; it just never registered. I inhaled deeply, filling my lungs to near bursting; the first free breath of a long-imprisoned man.

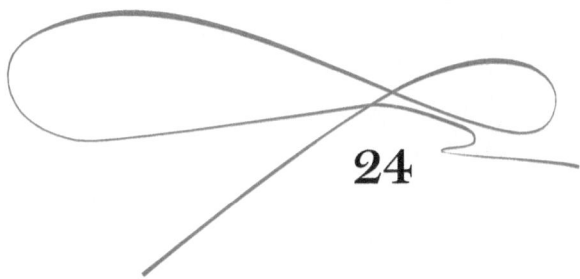

24

We rode a long stretch of river, finally stopping at a silty delta formed by a stream trickling down from the surrounding hillside. We beached our rafts, careful to watch our footing as we climbed out given Wiley's warning about the possibility of quicksand.

Wiley whistled for us to gather around. "Folks, this is the last fishin' hole you're gonna see on the Secret River," he said. The fishermen groaned in unison as if an off-key tenor section in a church choir. "Now, don't go gettin' your knickers in a twist," he said. "Before too long, the Secret joins up with the Nalunaq River. They'll still be good fishin', but this is about as good as it's going to get from here on in, especially for silvers."

"Hey Dad, we got a special request," Butch called out from his raft. He lounged back in his seat, a cigarette dangling from his grinning lips.

"What kinda special request?" Wiley said.

"Turns out that this here's Tyler Babcock's birthday!"

"No shit!" Zack shouted. "How the hell old are you?"

"The old boy's fifty-eight," Tony Giordano said, and slapped Babcock on his shoulder. From the creases at the sides of his eyes, his gray mustache and thinning gray hair, I would have figured Babcock was closer to seventy.

"I asked him what he wanted for his birthday," Butch said. "He told me that the best present we could give him is one of them silvers for dinner."

"Yeah, fuck this catch and release!" Cooper chimed in. "Look out there. There's gotta be hundreds of silvers in that hole, maybe thousands!"

I turned with the others toward the backwater bay downriver of the delta. A shadowy multitude of silver salmon swam lazily above the riverbed. Zack pointed at one that emerged out of the cloudy deep then circled quickly and dove back down upon spotting us. Even from that glimpse you could see the egg bulges at the sides. "Gettin' ready to spawn," Zack said. "Any day now."

"C'mon, Dad, it's our last night out here," Butch said. "How 'bout a fresh fish dinner to celebrate Tyler Babcock's birthday?"

Wiley stood tight-lipped, hands on his hips, head angled skyward. "All right, here's how it's going to work," he said. "Anybody catches a male, it's a keeper." A cheer went up from the fishermen with high-fives flying all around. Wiley quieted them with a shrill, two-finger mouth whistle. "All we're lookin' for is two males, that's it. Females get released. Got it?"

"Tell you what," Babcock said. "The first one to haul in a keeper gets a spot on my show!" Babcock smiled at Wiley as the others stampeded to the water's edge, rods cocked and ready to cast.

I was disappointed when Carl Cooper brought in the first fish, a magnificent salmon weighing at least fifteen pounds. He whooped as he held his struggling prize out in front of him, suspended from the hook deeply embedded in its top lip.

"Throw that God-damn thing back!" Wiley shouted. "What'd I say about keepers? Only males, right? This look like a male to you? You think a male carries eggs like this?" He ran his palms over the bulging sides of the fish. "Put her back before you do her some damage."

Cooper froze, his hands grasping the line from which the thrashing fish dangled. And then its lip tore away, the ruined salmon landing with a sickening thud on the wet, sandy ground. Cooper stared at it for a moment as it writhed on the beach, then kneeled to pick it up. Before he could get his hands on it, Wiley pushed him out of the way, toppling Cooper onto his back. "What the fuck?" Cooper said.

"*What the fuck*?" Wiley shouted. He squatted over the flapping fish, pointing to its gaping, broken mouth. "*This* the fuck!"

"Sorry," Cooper said. "You want me to throw it back, I'll throw it back."

Wiley rammed his fingers into one of the gills, lifted the fish and headed up the beach, away from the river. "Hey, where you going with my catch?" Cooper shouted.

"Your catch?" Wiley said as he stormed past. "Ain't your catch no more."

Wiley stopped at a jumble of driftwood near the forest's edge and pulled out a piece about two feet long. "Yo, boys!" he shouted. Butch and Zack came to his side at a quick trot. Wiley handed the fish to Butch, informing him what needed to be done with a grim look, a subtle motion of his head. Butch nodded, set the fish down and squatted above it, its tail between his legs. He quieted it with a firm hand just behind its dorsal fin as Wiley dropped to one knee at the head of the fish. He raised the driftwood club high and brought it down fast, striking the fish just behind its eyes with a sickening, hollow knock. The fish went rigid at the impact as if electrocuted. Wiley paused for a silent moment before ramming the club into the silt. He stood and again took up the fish by its gill, the flap of its upper lip dangling grotesquely from its gaping mouth.

Cooper picked himself up off the beach and brushed the grit from his waders as Wiley walked past. "At least it got us halfway to dinner," Cooper said, smiling at his buddies.

Wiley stopped. He laid the fish down, snatched up Cooper's fly rod and splintered it over his knee. "Pull that shit again and it'll be the last time you put a fly in the water on this trip," Wiley said. He drew back his fist but apparently thought better of it, lifted the fish and headed toward the river.

"I'm going to sue that asshole," Cooper said. "He owes me a new rod. Damn lucky I brought a second one with me."

"Dude, get a life," Babcock said. He set off toward the spawning ground, the other fishermen trailing close behind.

Kathy and I followed Wiley, Zack, and Butch down to the river. Wiley squatted at the water's edge and rinsed the sand and pebbles off the glistening silver skin of the fish as if giving it last rites. Butch brought a carabiner as large as his hand and a spool of wire from one of the rafts. Wiley threaded the wire through the eye on the back of the clip and tied it tight. He jammed the bar of the carabiner through the gills of the fish and out the damaged side of its mouth. He closed the clip, hoisted the fish by the line and set it down in the river then tied the free end of the wire through a grommet on the backside of the nearest raft. "That'll keep her," he said. He bent to rinse his hands, wiping them dry on his chest waders as he strode out of the river. "I just hope someone catches a male, quick," he said. "We need to get the hell out of here."

They continued fishing, bringing in nothing but females. Wiley paced the beach up near the scrub, glancing at his watch, the fishermen, the sky. After about an hour went by, he froze the fishermen with a piercing whistle. "Next good-sized fish does it," he shouted. "Male, female—don't matter. Just get it done. We gotta move."

I set down my notebook, took up my rod and stood at the far end of the fishermen on the soggy delta. While I had no interest in appearing on Babcock's show, I knew that it would be a dream for Larry; my plan was to give him the honor if I landed the keeper.

Kathy stood just to the right of me, casting with a rhythm as pure and beautiful as I remembered from that day back at the airport. Angie fished alongside of her, Butch standing with his arms around her back, the two of them holding the pole together, smiling, swaying with the rhythm of the rod, the line arching high above their heads, their effort climaxing in a graceful lunge forward atop the churning water. And then the fly disappeared, the rod nearly bending in two.

"We got one!" Angie screamed. Butch guided her as she brought the thrashing fish into the shallows. Zack splashed into the water and lifted it out of the river. "Fifteen pounds at least!" he said. Angie took hold of Butch's chin and kissed him hard.

"Looks like we got us a new star for the show," Babcock said, laughing.

The salmon was huge, her silver flanks ballooning outward with an enormous cache of eggs. Wiley strode over gripping the killing club, his hard, blank stare suggesting he was an unwilling executioner. He dropped to the ground and steadied the fish between his knees. He raised his arm high. Kathy turned her head at the sound of the harsh, hollow knock, the fish going rigid. "That's done," Wiley said. "Let's get going."

Zack clipped the second fish to our raft. The two salmon trailed behind us in the river, looking more alive than dead, as Wiley sat silent and glum, guiding us down the last stretch of the Secret River.

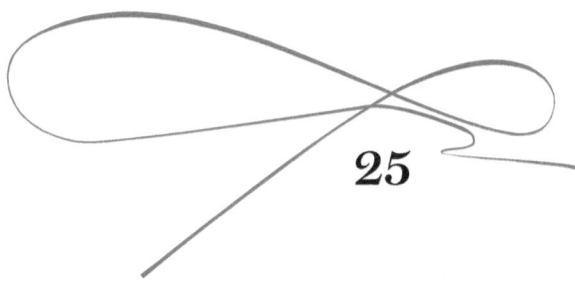

25

I felt the sound before I heard it; a dull vibration shaking the stillness of the afternoon air, coming from somewhere beyond a sharp leftward bend in the river. The rumble grew stronger with each passing second. Kathy laid her rod down and looked my way with uncharacteristically frightened eyes. "White water," Wiley said as if reading our minds. "Nothin' to worry about."

I figured that if whatever was up ahead was real trouble, Wiley would have asked us to stop fishing and pull the salmon on board until we got past it. I slid over and took hold of Kathy's hand. "Just some rapids," I said. "Should be fun."

Wiley worked the oars hard as we came around the bend. He fought the leftward pull of the current, straining to pull us across to the slower water on the right. The rumble had become a dull roar. "Put down your rods, pull in them fish and sit tight!" Wiley shouted.

Larry hauled the salmon on board, flopping them down at his feet. Kathy pressed up against me, her arms encircling my waist, mine wrapped around her shoulders. Larry dropped to a knee alongside the fish. The left side of the river collapsed into a funnel of water disappearing over a rocky ledge. Wiley strained at the oars, struggling to steer us to the right, the raft crashing through one then another then a third set of rapids, spinning and bending as waves spilled in over the sides.

We came to rest in a broad piece of quiet river, the spent force of the water thundering down from the rapids nudging us gently toward the far bank. Looking back upstream I could see the rapids—and the waterfall alongside. A straight pitch down, fifteen or so feet, onto a pile of boulders at the bottom. "You never said anything about a freaking waterfall," Larry said.

"Ain't worth talking about," Wiley said. "You hit them falls and you're dead, no matter how you cut it."

We waited in the quiet eddy, watching nervously as Zack's raft steered clear of the falls and made it down through the rapids, Butch's raft not far behind. The rafts bumped up together in the still water. "That there's the end of the Secret River," Wiley said. "We're on the Nalunaq now. We ride this a little ways and then we get picked up and head back into the village."

"Don't tell me that the trip's almost over," Angie said.

"Sorry, but it's just the rest of today and tomorrow morning. Then we're done."

"But don't you worry, hon," Butch said. "Tonight's the best night of all. We got a beautiful camping spot, right on the tip of an island. Great fishin', great views of the mountains—it's just plain goddamn beautiful."

The rafts drifted apart. No one spoke; the song of our fly rods, the gentle splash of slow water cresting over rocks, birds warbling unseen in the branches of the aspens that lined the riverbanks making the only sounds. The river widened. We made our way past a series of forested islands, one with bare, rocky hills running down its center, looking like the rippling back of some mythical river creature swimming the river from a time long past.

Not too long after, the river took a bend to the right. Another island came into view. Two stunted pines atop a rocky bluff faced us, clinging to a boulder with an interlocking web work of weatherworn roots. "That's our island," Wiley said. He steered us to the left, the river shallower here, the rocks on the bottom visible through the clear, slow-moving water. He docked the oars, allowing the raft to drift in the gentle current.

We floated alongside the island, the bluffs giving way to a wide, sandy beach. Behind the beach, a thin growth of low scrub bordered a grove of white-trunked aspen, their golden leaves fluttering in the gentle breeze. And then Wiley stood up, his eyes narrowed. He tilted his head back and sniffed the air.

I caught the scent as well—smoke. I looked downstream. A thin, gray column drifted up into the sapphire sky from the far end of the island.

"Dang it!" Wiley said and stomped his foot against the wood-plank floor. He sat back down, rowed us away from the island and stopped us dead in the river. He signaled the approaching rafts to regroup. Butch's raft bumped up against us, followed by Zack's.

"What's up?" Zack said.

"Somebody's at our camp," Wiley said. He pointed to the column of smoke.

"Son of a bitch," Zack said. He sniffed the air. "There's goddamn meat on that fire."

"Fucking T.J.," Butch said. "It's gotta be. He hunts along the Nalunaq, he knows about this place—"

"And I warned him to stay the hell out," Wiley said. He docked the oars, closed his eyes, tented his fingers before his face, momentarily resembling a red-bearded, floppy-hatted Buddha. He took a deep breath and lowered his hands. "Maybe I'm wrong. Maybe it's just some other fishing guide who doesn't know better."

"It's T.J.," Butch said. "I just know it."

"And if it is, we'll deal with it," Wiley said. "Not sure how, but we will. For now, just stay by me. Keep the oars up, let the river carry us quietly. I want to get a good look before whoever's there sees us—and *no fishing*!"

Wiley sat back down, eyes downriver, fingers twitching on the oar handles. The other rafts drifted with us, no one saying a word.

As we floated silently downriver, I couldn't help but think that this was all a lot of paranoid nonsense. Why would Wiley suspect that T.J. and the hunters would have taken over their campsite? Alaska is immense beyond reckoning; the hunters could be hundreds of miles away, shooting caribou or moose or whatever else they killed to make themselves happy. Why couldn't it be some group of fishermen occupying the campsite for the same reasons that Wiley stopped there when he first found it? How can Wiley claim ownership of a spit of sandy beach on an island in the middle of a river in a state bigger than most of the world's countries? It all seemed absurd.

We drifted closer. Flames flared from within a fire pit on the beach. Men moved between the fire and three tents set up near the first growth of aspen. We drew close enough to see their faces—the fucking hunters!

T.J. stood near the fire, tending slabs of sweet-smelling meat. Three of the others sat on stones set up around the far side of the fire. They smoked cigars and passed a bottle around, each taking a swig before handing it off. I could hear sounds of their conversation but couldn't make out any of the words.

"Motherfuckers stole our campsite," Zack whispered from a trailing raft. "I'm gonna kill 'em." Wiley pressed a finger to his lips and gestured for him to stay down. One of the hunters handed the bottle to T.J. He pulled his cigar from his mouth, took a long drink, wiped his lips with the back of his hand. He put the bottle down on the beach, glanced upriver, pointed our way. We'd been spotted.

"Hey there, Wiley," T.J. shouted. "Funny seein' you again way out here."

"You stole our campsite, you motherfucker!" Zack shouted.

"I don't see no reservation," T.J. said. "Show me your reservation and it's all yours."

A fusillade of profanities flew between our armada and the hunters as we drifted closer. Kathy grabbed my shoulder. "Look," she said, and pointed. Skins of grizzlies draped a log laid out between two boulders: one adult and two cubs.

"They shot cubs, Wiley," I said.

"I know," he said.

"Is that legal?"

"*Legal?*" he said like I was out of my mind for even asking.

Wiley stuck his fingers in his mouth and loosed a whistle that could have brought down the walls of Jericho. The battlefield fell silent. "It's bad enough that you go and take our campsite, but what the hell you doin' shootin' cubs and their mother?" Wiley shouted.

"Ain't your business what we shoot, just like it ain't my business what you catch," T.J. said. "Now go on and get the hell outta here before there's trouble—which, for the record, I don't want. There's some decent places to set up camp about a mile or two downstream. Not as good as this, but you can't have everything."

"You son of a bitch," Zack shouted. "If I was anywhere close to you, I'd break your fucking neck!"

"Well, then, looks like it's lucky you're out there floatin' away," T.J. said. "You take two steps close to me on this here beach, and it'd be the last two steps you'd take on God's holy earth."

"Tell you what, T.J.," Wiley said. "We're going to take your advice and move on down the river some—"

"What the fuck?" Zack shouted.

Wiley signaled for quiet and turned back toward T.J. "But, as far as trouble's concerned, I'd say you got that wrong," he said. "There's gonna be plenty of trouble for you, and everybody on your little trip, when the game marshals come for you. What's this now, your third violation? Killing cubs two years ago, shooting grizzlies from a helicopter last year? Now this? I'd say you can give your license one big, sloppy kiss good-bye. Same with your clients. And T.J., did you tell 'em about the fines?"

"Fines?" the hunter standing next to T.J. said. "What the fuck's he talkin' about?"

"Lemme put it this way," Wiley said. "You can forget about doin' any huntin' here in Alaska for the next twenty years or so, 'cause after they take your licenses away, you ain't getting them back any time before then. And after they fine you a hundred grand for each of them cubs you slaughtered, and you hire some expensive lawyers to keep your asses out of jail, I'm guessin' you ain't gonna have enough in your bank accounts to get back up here in your lifetime anyways."

"A hundred grand?" another hunter said.

"A hundred grand for *each of them cubs*," Wiley said. "Per person. State government'll make good use of it. Better than taxes."

"Like hell they will!" The fat-faced asshole who nearly had his arm disarticulated by Garrett back in Nalunaq came crashing through the underbrush, buckling up his pants. "I've been listening to this bullshit long enough!" He stumbled over to the log where they had leaned their guns and took hold of a shotgun. "Tax this, motherfuckers!" He aimed the gun toward our raft.

I dove on top of Kathy just before hearing the gun go off. I heard a couple of splashes, felt a hard *thunk* shake the raft. I raised my head and looked around. Larry and Rick Garrett were in the river on the far side of the raft, treading water. Wiley lay face down on the floor of the raft, his hands covering his head.

"You crazy fucker!" Zack screamed. "If I see you again, I'll kill you, I swear to God!"

T.J. grabbed the gun away. "Just get the hell outta here before somebody gets hurt," he said. "Just get."

Wiley and I hauled Larry and Garrett aboard, river water gushing into the raft from inside their waders. "Let's go!" Wiley shouted. He gave a tug on the oars, sending us downstream, the other rafts following close behind.

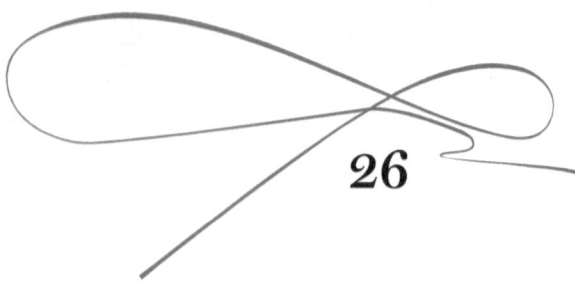

26

Wiley rowed us over to a sandy cove just beyond a big leftward bend in the river a few hundred yards past the end of the island. Zack and Butch beached their rafts alongside ours. "Everyone okay?" Wiley said.

"Great," Larry said. His hair was plastered to his scalp, his shirt dripping. "Just fucking great." Garrett, too, was soaked to the skin but said nothing.

"Why the hell didn't you let us take the bastards?" Zack said.

"'Cause they got guns, if you didn't notice," Wiley said.

"We got a gun, too."

"We got one, they got five. We're bobbin' around on the water, they're anchored to dry land. I'd say the advantage was with them. Besides, takin' a campsite ain't worth a shootin' war."

"We camping here for the night?" Russ asked.

Wiley looked around. "Might as well. It's a decent beach. We can set up a fire over there."

"A fire?" Babcock said. "I thought we don't make fires."

"It's your birthday, right?" Wiley said. "Besides, it's our last night and we've got fresh salmon. So yeah, we need a fire.

But I don't want no ashes left behind. When we leave here tomorrow morning, it's like we've never been here, got it?"

"Got it," Babcock said.

Larry and Garrett pulled some dry clothes from their duffels, headed through the scrub and into the forest. Kathy, Zack, and I gathered some stones and built a fire ring out on the beach alongside a couple of fallen tree trunks that would do nicely as seats. Some of the others went into the forest to gather wood. Zack set flat rocks on the sand in the middle of the fire ring. He put larger stones on either side, setting them there as rests for the logs we'd be cooking on. Before long, the others began returning with armfuls of wood. Butch and Angie came back, Butch dragging behind him a couple of gray-barked branches, dried needles still attached. "White pine!" Zack said.

"Damn straight!" Butch said, sounding like he'd just discovered buried treasure. He built a teepee of the white pine on the stones, breaking off some twigs and piling them at the base. He lit his cigarette lighter and held the flame to the twigs. Fire spread through the pile as if it had been doused by kerosene. Zack laid some of the bigger branches on top of the conflagration. "We'll let it burn good and hot for a while, give your brother and Garrett a chance to warm up."

The aroma of hot coffee drifted over the campsite. Everyone gathered around the steaming pot—except Larry and Garrett. Zack noticed their absence as well. Zack, Kathy and I walked to the edge of the forest. "Hey Larry, Rick, come get some coffee and warm your asses by the fire," Zack shouted. There was no response, not even sounds of footsteps on the carpet of twigs and leaves.

"Hey Larry!" I yelled. "Where the hell are you? You guys still alive?"

I was about to head in and look for them when I heard their footsteps coming toward us. "Where did you guys disappear to?" I said to Larry as he trudged out of the forest. "I was worried you might've gotten eaten by a bear or something."

Larry didn't smile at this. He had a hard look about him. I'd seen that look only one time before, the day he went into the hospital for his bone marrow transplantation. Back then, it seemed like a good look, a look of determination to get through it all and move on. Now it was different. I glanced over at Garrett and saw a look that was even harder. "What's going on?" I said.

"Nothing, bro," Larry said.

"Please don't bullshit me."

Larry said nothing before heading off toward the fire with Garrett.

"What the hell was that all about?" Zack said.

"Damned if I know."

"Well, something's up," Kathy said.

Wiley's whistle pierced through the campsite. "Yo, Zack," he called out. "Better get them salmon ready."

Kathy and I followed Zack down to the rafts. He unclipped the salmon and handed one to me. He was going to carry the other one himself, but Kathy put out her hands. Zack nodded, smiled, handed her the salmon with the torn mouth. He stepped inside the raft and pulled a leather-sheathed hunting knife out from beneath his seat.

Kathy and I carried the salmon toward the fire, holding them by the gills as we crossed the beach. The fish grew heavy, the gills sharp even through our gloved palms as we waited while Zack gathered some flat rocks, rinsed the grit off of them in the river and laid them on sand near the fire; an altar for the cutting of the fish.

A breeze carried the warmth of the fire toward us, rich with the scent of burning pine. Someone threw another branch of white pine into the blaze. The needles glowed golden and exploded in flame, the wood popping and crackling, the flames shooting higher than my head. Zack took the salmon from us and laid them on the stones, their eyes and skin glistening golden in the firelight, their flanks bulging with eggs.

We squatted down as the others gathered around. Zack rolled the fish with the torn mouth onto its back. He unsheathed his knife, stuck the point into its ventral slit and cut upward, slicing open its smooth underbelly. A thick, reddish flow oozed from the incision, eggs floated like red pearls inside the oily-looking liquid. Butch knelt between Kathy and me, one knee in the damp sand. "She was ready," Zack said. "Woulda laid these here eggs in a coupla hours. You can tell 'cause they're loose inside her." He brought some of the roe out on the side of the blade. "Any takers?"

The fishermen looked at each other, grinning nervously. "Thanks, but I take my eggs easy over," Babcock said.

"Well if he ain't eating it, I ain't eating it," Cooper said. "Gimme a holler when you got the meat cooked. I'm going fishing." He and most of the others headed back to the river. Wiley returned to the coffee warming on the camp stove.

Butch thrust a hand into the fish's belly and scooped out a handful of the roe. His eyes lingered on Angie's as the blood red roe dripped from his cupped hands, his face breaking into a smile. He brought his hands to his mouth and poured the roe onto his tongue; Angie shuddered and flashed a look of disgust. "Pretty damn good," Butch said through red-stained lips. "Inuits say it's an aphrodisiac."

Butch scooped out some more and held it out toward Angie. Her panicked eyes shot to Kathy. Kathy shook her head, her lips mouthing a silent "*no!*" Angie seemed to shrug, her expression now seeming more helpless and resigned than afraid. She closed her eyes and opened her mouth. Butch let the roe slide down his fingers onto Angie's outstretched tongue. She closed her mouth around it, her face expression-less, eyelids tightly shut. She worked the roe inside her mouth, her tongue's efforts traceable by the migrating bulge in her cheeks. She opened her eyes, grinned, took Butch's chin in one hand and laid a heavy kiss on him, their lips parting for a moment, allowing a stream of roe to escape her mouth and dribble onto Butch's beard.

Zack dipped his knife back into the open belly of the fish and held out the blade flat side up, covered with the roe. "Doc?" he said. I shook my head and glanced at Kathy. She motioned to Zack, took hold of his wrist and brought the edge of the blade to her tongue. Zack wiped a finger down the blade, spilling the roe into her mouth. She closed her lips and swallowed. "Not horrible," she said. She slipped off her gloves, reached inside the fish, scooped out more roe and held it out to me on two red-dripping fingers. I took her fingers in my mouth—salty, oily. I rolled the eggs up against my palate, pressing them with my tongue until they popped in small, salty explosions. Kathy touched two red fingers to her lips then on mine and smiled.

Then Garrett did something that seemed strange, even for Garrett. He handed Zack an empty coffee can. "How 'bout some in here?" he asked.

"In the can?" Zack said. Garrett nodded. "What the hell you want it for? Can't take it with us."

"Just do it," Garrett said.

Zack scooped out all the roe from the butchered salmon. It filled about a third of the can. "Happy?"

"The other one, too," Larry said.

Zack shrugged. He jabbed his knife through the skin of the second fish, sliced it open and scooped a handful into the can. "All of it," Larry said. Zack looked at my brother like he'd lost his mind. He scooped out all the roe from the second salmon and dropped it in.

"Don't go puttin' that in your tent overnight," Zack said. "It'll attract every grizzly between here and Anchorage." Larry shot Zack a curt salute before he and Garrett took the can and headed up the beach.

"Garrett's one strange dude," Zack said.

"War will do that to you," Kathy said. "I wonder what they're up to."

"Don't know," I said, "but you've got to think that Garrett didn't appreciate getting shot at again."

"That's for damn sure," Zack said. "Your brother, neither, especially when it ended them up in the river."

Butch clapped Zack hard on his brawny shoulder. "Let's stop pissin' around and get these silvers on the fire," Butch said.

They grilled the salmon and served it with canned corn Wiley had warmed on the stove. Then everyone sang *Happy Birthday* to Babcock; everyone, that is, except Larry and Garrett. I could tell from Larry's silence, from the way that he and Garrett gazed up the river toward the hunters' camp, that something weighed on their minds. Kathy noticed, too.

"Did you find out what's up with your brother?" she said after we'd finished dinner.

"Nothing," I said. "Your guess is as good as mine."

"Something's definitely going on."

"The gunshot might have pushed Garrett over the edge."

"He didn't have far to go," Kathy said. "He probably has PTSD from getting blown up in Iraq. Now he goes on vacation in Alaska and gets shot at again? Jesus!"

"At least we've left those crazy-ass hunters behind," I said.

"Not that far behind." Kathy nodded upstream. The smoke of the hunters' fire drifted up over the trees into the darkening sky.

"You think they're planning something?"

"Garrett and your brother? I don't know. Those asshole hunters almost screwed up this whole trip. Then they go and kill that bear and her cubs, steal our campground, and take a shot at us for good measure. Honestly, I wouldn't mind sticking it to them if I had the chance."

"So maybe we get the chance when we get back to Nalunaq. Report them to the game warden."

"Maybe," Kathy said in a way that seemed more unsettling than convincing.

Larry was in his sleeping bag when I returned to the tent. His hands were clasped behind his head, elbows out, staring into space. His eyes didn't move when I crawled inside. "Hey," I said. "No fishing tonight?"

"Nope."

I stripped down, pulled on my long underwear, climbed into my sleeping bag. The scent of roe hung heavy inside the tent. "That can's not in here?" I said.

"I guess my hands still smell. Sorry."

I hope the grizzlies can figure that out, I thought. "I guess this is our last night camping," I said.

"Guess so."

"Sorry we never saw the lights."

"Yeah, but no big deal. We caught fish. That's what it's about."

I sat up, took hold of my down vest, and packed it into the stuff sack for my sleeping bag. I set it down and laid my head on it. "You going to sleep now?"

"Gonna try."

"Larry?"

"Yeah?"

"You're not going to do anything stupid. With Garrett."

"Don't know what you're talking about, bro."

"The hunters—"

"Fuck the hunters."

"Just don't do anything stupid."

"Nothing to worry about, bro," he said in that way that made me think there was plenty to worry about. "Sleep tight."

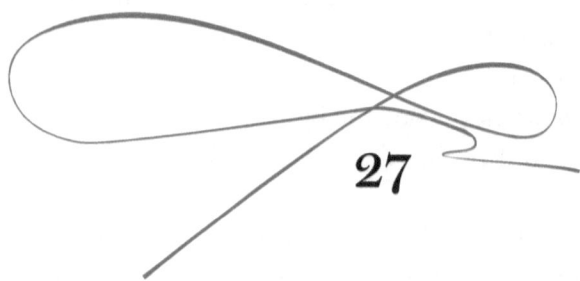

27

I closed my eyes, fighting the concerns swirling through my brain. I drifted out of consciousness into gray, hazy sleep, and then into a dream—a women's voice, soft but urgent, whispering my name. A zipping sound, a hand feeling the end of my sleeping bag, grabbing at my foot. Squeezing and shaking. I sat bolt upright.

"What the hell—?"

"Shh, it's me."

"Kathy?"

"Quiet! Something's up."

"Something's up? What do you mean—?"

"*Shhhh!*"

I blinked my eyes against the darkness, put my hand out and touched Larry's sleeping bag. Empty. "Where's Larry?"

"Out. With Garrett."

"What the hell time is it?"

"Around two-thirty."

"What's he doing with Garrett at two-thirty?"

"Not just Garrett. I think Butch and Zack are in on it, too."

I rubbed my face awake, Kathy silhouetted against the moonlight bathing the tent walls. "In on what? What's going on?"

"I don't know. I got up to pee, went back to my tent and couldn't get back to sleep. Then I heard footsteps and whispers. Larry and Garrett went over to Butch and Zack's tent. The four of them headed to the beach."

"You heard all this?"

"Heard and saw; I watched them in the moonlight from inside my tent. Zack said something about getting those motherfuckers. He's not the best whisperer."

"Oh, shit."

"Let's go."

"Go where?"

"See what's going on."

I sighed, yawned, stretched. I could tell that Kathy was going whether or not I did. "Let me find some clothes." I reached for my headlamp.

"Don't turn on your light!" she said. "Wear what you're wearing."

"My long johns?"

"That's what I've got on."

"Seriously?"

"It's not that cold out."

"For Alaska, maybe."

I crawled out of the tent after Kathy and reached for the tent zipper. "Don't!" she whispered. "And leave your sandals, it's mostly sand. Just stay quiet."

Kathy took hold of my hand. We scurried up the beach, our heads low, our steps quick and silent. A nearly full moon hung in a clear sky. The beach took on an other-worldly glow, the sand blue, scattered boulders casting shadows in the half-darkness, the river glimmering like something electric. We made our way soundlessly out of the camp and around the bend. The hunters' island came into view across the river, a long, dark shadow in the moonlight.

We crept closer. Four figures stood on the beach just before us, paired off in twos, shirts off, their moon shadows stretching across the sand. They passed something between them. I squinted and recognized it as the coffee can that Larry and Garrett had filled with salmon roe. Larry stuck his hand in the can, scooped something out, smoothed whatever it was over Garrett's shoulders and back. Zack reached into the can and splattered the contents onto Butch's back.

"What the fuck?" I whispered. Too loudly.

Garrett spun on his heels and snatched his hunting knife off the beach. "Who's there?" he whispered.

"It's me—David," I said.

"David!" Larry whispered. "Goddamn it!"

"And Kathy," she said.

"Oh, Christ!"

"What the hell are you guys up to?" she whispered to the four shirtless men. Garrett lowered his knife as we came closer. Nauseating scents of fish and wet charcoal filled the air. "And what's that awful smell?"

"Doesn't matter," Larry said. "Go back to sleep."

I glanced across the river. We stood about one hundred yards downstream from the hunters' camp at the tip of the island. "You're not thinking—?"

"We're not thinking about anything, except that you two need to head back to camp. Let us do what we need to do."

"Larry's right," Garrett said. "Head back into camp. Let us do our job."

I noticed other knives stuck blade-first into the sand. "Your job?" I said. "What are you going to do, slit their throats while they're asleep? Are you guys out of your fucking minds?"

"No one's getting their throats slit, much as I'd love to do it," Garrett said. "We're just going to teach them a lesson."

"What kind of lesson?" Kathy said.

"That you don't go stealing somebody else's campsite," Butch said.

"That you don't fuck up somebody else's vacation so you can bring liquor on your trip," Larry said.

"That if you fire a gun at somebody, you damn well hit 'em, or they're goin' to come back and make you pay," Garrett said.

"You *are* out of your fucking minds," I said.

"We come out of the river, do our business, and disappear back into it," Garrett said. "We do it right and those pricks won't know anything until they wake up in the morning."

"After we've broken camp and are long gone," Zack added.

"Come out of the river?" I said. "You're swimming across?"

"The channel's shallow," Zack said. "You can mostly walk it."

"Why not take a raft?" Kathy said. She sounded engaged. This wasn't good.

"No way," Garrett said. "Too exposed. Like I said, we slide on out of the river, do our business, disappear back into it. End of story."

"What business?" Kathy whispered.

"I'm taking out their guns," Garrett said. "They ain't goin' to be shooting at much of anything anymore, at least not on this trip."

"And I'm dumping their liquor," Larry said.

The moonlight lit up Butch's and Zack's grins. "What's your assignment?" I asked.

"Me and Zack are security," Butch said.

"In case any of those fuckers wake up and try to cause trouble," Zack added. "Which I kind of hope they do."

"If they wake up, we've fucked up the mission," Garrett warned. "We're going to be quick, quiet, efficient. Over and back. Got it?"

"Got it, commander," Butch said and smiled at me.

"You're forgetting something," Kathy said. "Those cubs they killed. The mother, too."

"They'll be done killing when I finish with their guns," Garrett said.

"But they'll get new guns," Kathy said. "Then they'll come back and kill some more. We've got to stop them."

We? I covered my face with my sandy hand.

"How do we do that?" she said.

"Report 'em, like my dad said," Butch answered.

"But to make it stick, don't you need evidence?" Kathy said.

"Damn," Butch said. "Didn't think of that."

"What about one of those pelts? Evidence enough?" Kathy said.

"I guess," Butch said.

"We don't have the time or the hands to fuck with any pelts," Garrett said. "Everyone already has an assignment. We gotta be in and out, quick!"

"I'll grab a pelt," Kathy said.

I stared at her in the moonlight. "Are you crazy?" I whispered.

"Why crazy? I'll go with them and bring back one of the cub pelts. We'll take it to the authorities in Nalunaq. That'll nail them."

"But we can't prove that those assholes killed it," Butch said. "They'll break camp and be long gone before anyone comes for 'em."

"What if we strand them?" Kathy said. "Sink their rafts. Send the authorities up here from Nalunaq. They'll get nailed red-handed."

"You want to leave them on that island with no food, no way to get out?" I said. "What are you thinking?"

"With all the meat they got, and the fish in the river, they ain't going to starve," Butch said. "Besides, we're only half a day's float from our take-out point, and then about another hour from Nalunaq in a boat. State police could be up here in about two hours with a motored dinghy."

"You really think the cops are going to come all the way up here on our word alone?" Larry said.

"That's why we need to bring them one of those cub pelts," Kathy said. "Evidence."

"She's got a point," Butch said.

"What if they ditch the rest of them?" I said.

"No way," Butch said. "They came all the way here for them trophies, they ain't getting' rid of 'em so fast. They'll be super pissed that we took one of 'em, probably thinkin' we wanted it for ourselves."

"It's a fucking great idea!" Zack said. "Let's grab a pelt, slash their rafts and strand those bastards!"

"All right," Garrett said. "We'll stick it to 'em, good."

Zack threw his fist into the air. "Yeah, baby!" he whispered.

Garrett signaled us to gather around. "Now listen up. We got a new mission; grab a pelt and sabotage their rafts. Fuckin' up their rafts comes last, 'cause it may make some noise. Me and Butch'll take care of the rafts when everyone else is back in the river. Kathy, if you're really serious about comin' along, your assignment is to secure a pelt."

"I'm definitely serious," Kathy said.

"Better wait 'till you hear the whole plan before you decide," Garrett said.

"I thought I just heard the plan."

"You did, for the mission. But here's the ops details."

"Ops?" I said.

"Operations," Larry said. "The logistics."

"We swim across, do what we need to do, come back," Kathy said.

"Quick, quiet, invisible," Garrett said. "*Invisible*," he emphasized. "That's what this is for." With the tip of his hunting knife, he pointed to the black paint on his face, to the black lines decorating his chest and burned arm.

"What is that stuff?" I asked. "It reeks."

"Charcoal from the fire," Larry said. "Mixed in with the salmon roe."

"What the hell?"

"The oil from the roe keeps the camouflage on our skin when we're in the water," Larry said.

"At least that's what Garrett says," Zack added.

"You ever hear an otter swim?" Garrett said.

"Not really," Kathy said.

"That's 'cause you can't. They're silent in the water. With all that oil on their fur, they just glide. Silent killers. That's what we're gonna be tonight, a band of otters, gliding across the river—quick, quiet, invisible." Garrett tossed his knife point-down in the sand near his feet. He pulled off his pants and stood naked in the moonlight. "Slick as otters," he said. "That's the way it's got to be." He toed the can toward my brother. Larry picked it up, dug out some of the slurry and began smearing it across the rest of Garrett's back and over his tight, white-skinned ass. "You still in?"

"Let's do it," Butch said. He and Zack stripped; Zack started to fingerpaint his brother's face.

"Kathy?" I whispered.

"I always liked otters," she whispered back. "I think they're cute." She turned back to the naked men. "I'm in," Kathy said.

"You're not serious," I whispered.

"Dead serious." She walked past Zack and picked up the can.

"Don't go running away with that," Garrett said.

"It'll be right here," she said. She headed a couple of steps up the beach and turned her back to the men. She glanced once over her shoulder and peeled off the top of her long johns, standing bare-breasted before me in the moonlight. "Okay, Picasso, get going," she said, and tossed her top onto the sand. "Start with the face, then work your way down."

I dipped two fingers in. It was like fishing around in a can of thick, gritty motor oil with a really bad smell. "Any particular effect you're after?" I whispered. "New age Amazon? Or are we feeling more Navy SEAL?"

"Not seal, David. Otter."

"Seal, otter, what the fuck's the difference?" I muttered. I touched her at the corner of her left eye, drew a thick line down until reaching her jawline, traced this around to the middle of her chin. I stuck my fingers back into the muck and drew a line mirroring the first one on the other side of her face. I painted lines curving beneath her eyes and over her cheeks, ending at the corners of her mouth. She closed her eyes and held back her bangs as I painted a thick stripe beginning dead center at her hairline and carried it straight down over the bridge of her nose.

"Good enough," I said.

She opened her eyes. "How do I look?"

"Like an otter. That needs an exorcist."

"Perfect."

"Hey, where's that can?" Larry said.

"I'll bring it to you," I said.

"How 'bout I come over and get it?" Zack said.

"Maybe not," I said. I brought the can to where the others were getting decorated for battle. "Take some quick, we may take a while."

"We ain't got a while," Garrett said. "Just get her done. We gotta move." He scooped out a handful of the stinking, black ooze and, using his palm as a palette, began painting my brother's face.

I headed back to Kathy and dipped my fingers into the can. "This is going to be cold," I whispered.

"Can't be much colder than I am now," she said.

I started at the side of her neck, drawing thick lines over her goose bump-covered shoulders, down the outside of her arms to her wrists. I drew smaller, down-angling lines extending out from the thick one, meeting on the soft flesh on the undersides of her arms as she held them out and away from her torso.

I walked around to her back. She flinched as I touched two fingers dripping with the cold, oily slurry to the nape of her neck, just below her hairline. I drew a line straight down her back, my fingers rising and falling over each bony prominence until stopped by the waistband of her long johns. "Wait," she said. She hooked her thumbs inside her bottoms, pulled them down and kicked them aside. "Well, that's done," she said.

I forked the line, extending it down over each buttock until ending at her heels, and then threw in some horizontal stripes across the backs of her buttocks and legs. And then I hesitated.

"Stop admiring your work and finish," Kathy said. "I'm not going through all this and then getting left behind."

I walked around front and faced her. She looked beautiful in the light of the nearly full moon, standing naked and still upon the glistening riverbank, a beauty that shone through despite her face being painted like an offering at a human sacrifice. She raised her chin as I placed my freshly dipped fingers upon her sternal notch and drew a line bisecting her sternum, carrying it down between her breasts, encircling her navel. She flinched when I touched the upper edge of her pubic bone. "You all right?"

"Yeah," she said, although you could see from the goose-bumps on her arms and the occasional waves of trembling that swept through her that the cold was getting to her. "I'm fine."

I put more of the gritty paint on my finger, striped her collarbones and chest. She lifted her arms and locked her fingers behind her head as I drew wavy stripes around each of her breasts. She was really shivering now, her entire body trembling. A glance over her upraised arm and I could see that the others were nearly finished. "Almost done," I said.

I knelt down in the sand, the mostly empty can in my hand. I dipped a single finger into the slurry and touched it atop her pubis. She flinched. I traced a line across the top edge of her pubic bone, the skin unexpectedly mounded, rough, irregular. Scarred. She took my hand and guided my finger once again across the scar—an imperfectly healed Caesarian section incision.

I rose up off the sand. Her hands caressed the sides of my head, easing me toward her until our foreheads touched.

"You have a child?"

I could feel her head shake.

"But—"

She eased off, touched her finger to my lips. "Not now," she said.

She crouched to pick up the can, dipped her finger in, drew a line down my nose. "What are you doing?" I whispered. She hushed me and drew lines across my cheeks.

"Your top," she said. "Quick."

"What?"

"You're coming, too."

"I don't think so."

Kathy leaned in toward me, her eyes locked on mine. "You remember how it was back in Nalunaq?" she said, her whisper harsh, emphatic. "Remember the pain they caused your brother, and you? Remember how they laughed? Sometimes a little revenge is a good thing, David. Therapeutic. Now strip!"

She stared at me, her fearsomely painted face glowing in the moonlight. I pulled off my top and slipped out of my bottoms. "Happy now?" Kathy kissed me. "I'll take that as a yes," I said.

"What the hell are you doing?" Larry whispered.

"David's coming, too," Kathy said.

"For fuck's sake," Larry murmured. "We ain't waiting," he said and followed the others to the river.

Kathy worked fast, striping my shoulders and back, buttocks and legs with quick, firm strokes of her fingers. "Sorry but I don't have time to be artistic," she said. She scooped out a handful of the stinking goop and splattered it on the center of my chest, spreading it this way and that through my chest hair. "Jackson Pollock meets the Green Berets."

"When I was a kid, I hated the idea of body painting," I said. "I couldn't even stand to have my face painted."

"Why doesn't that surprise me?" She knelt in the sand, tapped the back of her hand against my inner thigh. I shifted, spreading my legs at her signal. We were down to the dregs, more gritty charcoal than oily roe, the paint scratchy as Kathy decorated my groin and upper thighs. "You say you still hate body painting?"

"Yeah, I guess. Why?"

"'Cause it looks to me like Pinocchio is telling a fib," she said, and threw in one last, opportunistic stripe.

"*Oh, shit!*"

She bounced up to her feet and kissed me once again. "Don't worry," she whispered. "You'll be back to normal as soon as we hit that cold river water."

The others had already waded in by the time we reached the river's edge. They were up to their waists, their arms held high above them, each with a knife clasped in one hand, moonlight trembling on the surface of the disturbed river. My feet went numb as soon as they hit the water. "Mind over matter," Kathy said. "Don't think about it." We clasped hands and waded in together, the river bottom turning from soft sand to uncomfortable rock beneath my feet, the water icy around my ankles, calves, thighs. I scooped some water and splashed it on the back of my neck, shivering as it ran down my spine.

We waded in further, the water rising over my hips to the level of my navel, lapping at the bottoms of Kathy's black-striped breasts. "Mind over matter," she said breathlessly. "Mind over matter."

Each small step forward was torture. "Fuck this," I said.

"You can't go back now."

"Who's going back?" I closed my eyes and dropped down into the river. The sudden rush of cold took my breath away. I shot back up, mouth open, gasping.

"Quiet back there!" Garrett whispered. "Otters, remember?"

"That was brilliant," Kathy said, smiling through her war paint.

"Mind over matter," I said. Kathy squeezed my hand and disappeared into the river. She tugged on my arm and surfaced. The lines I had carefully applied on her face had run together, shading her skin in a Goth-like mélange of black streaks.

We caught up to them just short of the enemy shoreline. Garrett had stopped the landing party, his arm bent at the elbow, his hand balled into a fist. "Ready?" Garrett said in his softest whisper. Nods from Larry and Butch, a thumbs-up from Zack.

"Remember, nobody gets hurt," I said.

"Shucks, Doc," Butch whispered, "you spoil all our fun."

"Jesus Christ!" Garrett hissed. "You want to wake these fuckers up, go ahead and keep yackin'. *Then* someone's getting hurt. After this, no more words, got it?" We all nodded. "Okay, one more time. I'm taking out the guns. Larry, you go for the booze. Kathy, you and Doc grab a pelt but be careful about it, those suckers might be heavy. Butch and Zack, you keep watch. Somebody wakes up, you lay 'em out, but no permanent damage. Head straight for the river as soon as you're done. Me and Butch'll disable the rafts. If we spend two minutes out there, it's one minute too long. Got it?" Heads nodded. "All right, then—go!"

Our raiding party emerged zombie-like from the dark stillness of the river. Garrett headed toward the tents, Larry to the campfire pit where they'd set up their kitchen. Kathy took my hand. "Over here," she whispered. We headed toward the point of the island where we had seen the pelts, trailed by our moon shadows, sharp rocks in the sand slowing our progress across the beach. In the glow of the moon the pelts didn't take long to find. The skin of the mother bear lay splayed out alongside those of her cubs, heads dangling, eyes and mouths open. "Bastards," Kathy whispered.

A bottle shattered. We froze, my heart pounding. A light went on inside one of the tents. "Let's get the hell out of here," I whispered. I grabbed a pelt. Garrett was right, it was heavier than I'd imagined. I clutched it to my chest and ran as fast as I could, following Kathy back to the river. I tried to keep the pelt dry above my head, but it was too big and heavy and so set it down on the water. It was good to be back in the river, the water feeling strangely warm and safe after the chilly danger of the land.

We heard one of the tent flaps unzip. An arm stuck out, holding a flashlight. The beam swept across the camp. "Fuck you, fucking bears," T.J. called out, sounding drunk and sleepy. "Get the hell out or you'll end up like your cousins." With that, he turned off his flashlight and zipped up his tent.

Kathy lay low in the water beside me. "Where the hell is everyone?" she whispered.

"Probably sitting tight for a minute," I said.

"Probably scared shitless," Kathy said.

We remained quiet and still, waiting for one of those minutes that seemed like an hour. We heard soft footsteps on the beach, saw the shadowy body of a naked man hunched low and moving fast, entering the water with a gentle splash.

"Pssst," I whispered. "Over here."

"Oh man!" It was Larry.

"What happened?"

"One of the bottles slipped. Fucking fish oil."

"Where are the others?"

As if in answer to my question, Zack's naked body scurried crablike across the beach and into the river. "Holy shit, what the fuck was that?" he whispered as he glided up alongside us.

"Tell you later," Larry said. "Where are Butch and Garrett?"

"Headed down to the rafts."

The four of us laid low in the water, eyes peering out like submerged crocodiles. After another minute or so, Garrett and Butch crossed the beach and headed toward the rafts. We heard squeaks of knives cutting through rubber, the hiss of escaping air. "I sure hope T.J.'s gone back to sleep," I said.

A moment later they swam up alongside us. Butch held his knife in one hand, a jagged-edged oval of rubber in the other. "Like to see them try to patch that," he said and flung the palm-sized piece of rubber downstream. The piece that Garrett tossed away seemed even larger.

Garrett's eyes swept across us. Satisfied that all were present and accounted for, he signaled a return to base. He lowered himself into the river and drifted off with the current. I turned onto my side and half-swam, half-glided back toward camp, dragging the waterlogged pelt beside me, my hand clutching the back lower edge of the cub's jaw, its dead, blank eyes staring at me.

The swim back to camp seemed to take no time at all. The six of us emerged from the water, our skin smeared with what now had become a monotonal coat of oily charcoal gray. "We sure kicked their asses," Zack said. "Can't wait to write a poem about this!"

"Shut the fuck up, man," Butch said. "You want to wake up the whole camp?"

"We're going to have to wake them soon anyway," Garrett said. "We gotta get outta here early."

"What about breakfast?" Zack said.

"It'll have to wait."

"I don't get it," Zack said. "Those bastards are fucked. They ain't going nowhere any time soon."

"When they wake up, they're gonna know that it wasn't no bear that fucked them up," Garrett said. "I took out their guns, but they've still got knives. We don't want any more trouble with them. We gotta be gone before they figure it out and decide to swim on over here."

"Still a little ways to dawn," Butch said. "Guess we can let everybody sleep for another couple of hours."

"No more than that," Garrett said.

Larry crossed his arms across his chest and did a warming dance. "How do we get this oily shit off?" Larry said. "No way I'm getting back into my sleeping bag like this."

"I've got some soap back in the tent," Butch said. "C'mon."

Zack, Larry, and Garrett followed Butch back to camp. I turned to join them, but Kathy grabbed my hand. "Wait," she whispered.

They had gone a few steps before they realized that we hadn't followed. "What the hell are you two doing?" Larry whispered.

"Dealing with the pelt," Kathy said. "We'll be there in a bit."

"You need soap?" Butch said.

"I brought my own, thanks," she said.

We said nothing, shivering in the chill night breeze, waiting until the four naked men had trudged up the beach and disappeared around the bend. I toed the pelt, the fur cold, wet, and sandy. "What do you want to do with this poor guy?" I said.

Kathy crouched down and took hold of a rear paw. "Help me flatten it," she said. We tugged on the paws until the pelt lay smooth on the beach.

"We ought to hang this up on a branch if we want it to dry," I said.

She came around to where I stood, her face lit by the moon. "Later." She touched a finger to my forehead, slid it down my nose. "Still oily," she said.

She moved closer, brushed my lips with a kiss. "Do you really have soap?" I whispered.

She nodded. "Biodegradable."

She dropped to her knees on the pelt, tapped her hand on the wet fur. "Seriously?" I said.

"Why not?"

"On this? A little kitsch, no?"

"Better than having rocks digging into your back."

"*My* back?"

"Stop complaining."

I laid alongside her inviting hand, the fur cold and wet on my back. Wild-smelling. Kathy above me, her head thrown back, eyes closed, black-smeared neck, ribs, breasts shining in the soft blue light of the moon like something hewn from stone.

Afterward she collapsed at my side, our arms tight around each other, our legs intertwined. "You know we're insane?" I whispered.

"Definitely. So how does it feel to be a victorious warrior?" she whispered.

"I could get used to it."

Kathy settled her head on my chest and turned her face up to the moon. The sky already was losing its darkness, the black of night turning gray-blue in the east, only a fading few of the brightest stars still glimmering alongside two still-brilliant planets. Her body shook, a different kind of shaking from the cold shivers that the warm press of our bodies had overcome. I thought she might be laughing, but when I saw the glimmer of a tear I knew otherwise. I stroked her hair with my oily hand. "What's wrong?" I whispered. She squeezed me harder, took hold of my finger, traced the path of the C-section scar. "They did a nice job, don't you think?" she said. "Barely there."

"How old is your child?"

Kathy sighed, hugged me harder. "She would have been—let's see. A teenager. She would have been a teenager already."

Her use of the past tense landed like a punch to my gut. "A daughter," I said. "What is—what was—her name?"

"Jacqueline. I called her Jackie. Do we have to go into this?"

"Not if you don't want to." Her body tensed. She freed her leg, rolled over and suspended herself above me on outstretched arms, hands flat on the fur, her eyes locked onto mine.

"Okay, this is the story," she said in that breathless way people talk when a part of them wants the words out before another part of them makes them stop. "I was married, his name was Tyler. My brother's best friend, from college—"

"Another Princetonian?"

She touched a sandy finger to my lips. It tasted vaguely of

fish. "Let me finish. Yes, another Princetonian. They interned together, at Cantor Fitzgerald. Got jobs there, working with my dad. Everyone thought it was kind of funny when we got married. He had become like another brother to me. A little incestuous, you know what I mean? You already know how that story ended, for all of them. As for Jackie—I guess you could say she died that day, too."

"I remember something about a daycare center in one of the towers," I said, barely imagining it.

"Yeah, it was on one of the lower floors. All those kids made it out safely, thank God. My Jackie was safe and sound, right inside here." She placed a palm on her abdomen. "Seven months pregnant and watching it all on a TV in the waiting room with the rest of my patients that morning. Second floor, Beth Israel Hospital, up on 15th Street. I knew where their offices were. When I saw where the planes hit, I didn't need to make a phone call. I lost all three of them—my dad, my brother, my husband—just like that, David. Just like that. I didn't have to look twice, I just knew."

"Jesus."

"Jesus? He was AWOL that day. Still is, as far as I'm concerned."

I reached up, brushed a hand across her cheek. She lowered herself, her chest cold on mine. I kissed the top of her damp hair. "And Jackie?" I whispered.

"Jackie. Let's just say that that kind of experience isn't conducive to the successful completion of pregnancies. I'm not exactly sure what happened. I guess it was all those pictures of the lost all over the city. All the smoke and ash, me carrying around that baby imagining having to tell her or him—we chose not to know, we wanted to be surprised— that her father, grandfather, and uncle were incinerated in that hellhole. It felt like the end of the fucking world. I went into labor about a week later. I think my body just revolted at the idea of bringing a child into all that crazy shit. When they detected fetal distress, they went in and got her. Seven months, borderline viability. Survived about a week in the NICU. That's it." She kissed my shoulder. "Wait here."

"Where are you going?"

"Just wait here." She got up and hurried to her tent, returning a few moments later with her bottle of soap. "You blew me off once," she said. "Want a second chance?"

"My rain check?"

"Exactly."

"I thought I just cashed that one in."

"I'm feeling generous." She squirted a line of soap down the front of my chest and then her own. We stepped back into the river together, the bracing chill now familiar and strangely welcome. We washed until the oily black was gone. She soaped her hair, ducked beneath the water to rinse, then shampooed mine.

I dropped down into the river, rinsed off the soap and suspended myself in the chill waters, feeling like I was living in some bizarre dream. A hand caught my wrist and pulled me up. I was shivering hard. "We better get going before we get hypothermia," Kathy said.

We dried ourselves on our cast-off long johns before slipping back into them, the damp fabric providing welcome protection against the chill breeze. We lifted the waterlogged pelt, shook the sand off, carried it back toward camp and draped it over a boulder. "You know we're going to feel half-dead later today," Kathy said.

"The price of feeling totally alive right now."

"Hey David?"

"Yeah?"

"You think Zack's really going to write a poem about this?"

"I hope so," I said. "If he does, it'll be epic."

She smiled, squeezed my hand, kissed me once more. "See you in an hour or two," she said. She headed to her tent, unzipped the flap, and crawled inside.

I climbed as quietly as I could into my tent, trying my best not to wake Larry. I curled myself into a ball inside my sleeping bag, waiting for the heat of my shaking body to warm me.

Larry shuffled in his sleeping bag. "Hey, bro," he said.

"Hey."

"That was something, wasn't it?"

"It sure was."

"You're a warrior," he said. "I always knew you were a warrior, deep down. Dad knew it, too."

This last comment kind of threw me. My dad saw me as a warrior with words, a guerrilla for grades—hardly a soldier in the classic sense. "You're the real warrior," I said, meaning every word. "And you gave me an amazing gift."

"What the hell did I give you?" he said.

"An invitation to come on this trip—and maybe get my life back."

"I thought you were having a shitty time."

"Did I look like I was having a shitty time tonight?"

"No, I thought you looked great. Loved the war paint."

"You know what? So did I. Now I'm ready for a little sleep."

Larry shuffled again in his bag. "Hey David?"

"Yeah?"

"I wasn't bullshitting. About that warrior stuff from Dad."

"Thanks, nice to know." I rolled over. "You know, Dad and

Mom would've been happy to see us out here in Alaska, sleeping together like this," I said.

"I guess."

"I hope it doesn't take another twenty-five years before we do it again."

"I'll be lucky if I'm alive in twenty-five years."

"You'll be alive."

"Well, you're the hot-shot scientist, so I'll take your word for it."

"Goodnight."

"You, too."

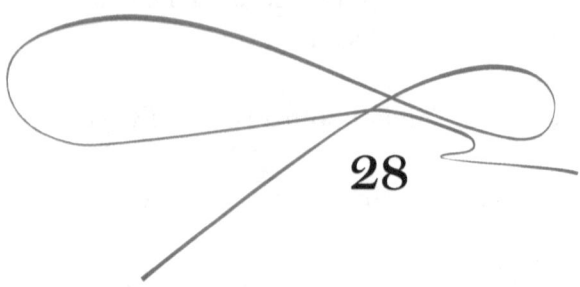

28

Larry and I woke to Zack's whistle. Larry murmured something from deep inside his bag, his words muffled by a cocoon of 800 fill-power goose down. I poked my eyes out of the small air hole I'd left for myself at the top of my bag. Zack unzipped our tent flap and stuck his head inside, looking like something stuffed and mounted over a fireplace. "Rise and shine, gentlemen," he said.

Larry's face emerged from the top of his bag. "Too early," he groaned.

"Not if we want to be outta here before them hunters wake up," Zack said. "Everybody else is awake. You all better haul ass."

I bumped into Kathy up near the shovels, she just coming out from the bushes, me in dire need of heading in. She smiled. "What?" I said.

"I think you've got the worst case of bed-hair I've ever seen." She ran her fingers over my scalp. It felt like my hair was standing in a crest running from ear to ear across the top of my head.

"And I've got to pee," I said. I licked my palm—still tasting fishy despite the liberal use of Kathy's biodegradable soap—and did my best to flatten out my hair. "Better?"

"Beautiful. Now go before you have an accident."

I finished and headed over to the group that had gathered around the cub pelt. Larry was now wide awake, regaling them with the story of our attack.

"Sounds like you fucked 'em up pretty good," Babcock said.

"They got what they deserved," I said. I stared at the pelt, the snout scraping the sand, the sharp-toothed mouth open in a silent cry, and felt that they didn't get close to what they deserved.

Wiley's whistle called our attention back to the rafts. Our campsite was bare, the tents and cooking gear stowed. "Let's walk the beach and get outta here," Wiley called.

I took hold of the paws on one side of the pelt, the damp fur smelling like a hairy dog that had just taken a swim in a filthy creek. Larry grabbed the paws on the other side. We headed over to the rafts, made some room in one of them, rolled the pelt up and stowed it. The others finished walking the beach and came toward us. Kathy came over and took my hand. "Ride with me?" I asked.

"Love to, but I don't think it's going to work. Angie wants my company. Your brother and Garrett are going to want to fish together. You definitely should stay with Larry considering this is the last stretch." She stood on her toes and kissed me. "Something to remember me by," she said.

We headed down to the rafts and pushed off. As we glided out into the current, I heard shouts coming from the hunters' camp, unintelligible echoes of impotent outrage dissipating into the wilderness. I glanced at Zack, sitting at the oars, a wide grin on his face. He flashed me a thumb's up, a signal I was happy to return.

The day dawned as perfect as the one on which we left Nalunaq almost a week before. In the warm brilliance of the

Arctic late-summer sun the events of the night seemed like a distant, crazy dream. I shed my layers one by one until I wore only a T-shirt above my waders. The fish seemed rejuvenated by the warmth and light; everyone caught rainbows and silvers.

After catching a few of my own, I set down my rod for the last time, pulled out my notepad and began writing about the events from the previous day. This time, no one got on my case for giving up precious fishing time. Zack, Larry, even Garrett chimed in, recalling each detail of our attack. No one had to remind me about taking the bear pelt, its dead eyes gazing up at me from the floor of the raft as I jotted my recollections.

By about noon the river had widened, sweeping us through broad bends and curves overhung with eroding cliffs of flood- and ice-cut earth. Zack navigated us around the final bend of our ride. We beached the rafts on a sandy peninsula blanketed with wildflowers, pansy-like blossoms of red, blue, yellow, orange, and purple dancing in the breeze. After we unloaded all the gear, Zack and Butch deflated the rafts and stacked them at the water's edge. There was a bittersweet sadness to it all that comes with the end of something; a sadness I could not have imagined feeling after those first couple of days of the journey.

Kathy and I stripped off our waders in favor of the shorts we had on underneath. We nestled together on the warm sand, my head resting upon a river-smoothed stone. Kathy settled her head on my stomach, I stroked her sun-warmed hair. "My mother grew pansies in her garden, right outside our back door," I said. "In the spring, we'd come home from school, Larry and me, and there would be all these pansies. I'm not sure these are pansies though."

Kathy reached out, picked a purple one and held it between her thumb and forefinger. "I hereby declare this a pansy, in honor of your mom," she said. I accepted her gift and slid the stem through her hair above her ear.

"She would have wanted you to have it," I said. "Besides, this looks better than war paint."

Kathy smiled and settled her head back upon me. "A time and purpose for everything."

"Under heaven. Where's Angie?"

"Off with Butch."

"Taking a walk?"

"Or whatever."

"Whatever sounds kind of nice right now."

"Yes, it does," she said. She rolled onto her side, shifted her head higher up on my chest, her face toward the river. We watched Larry fishing with Babcock and some of the others, their lines swishing golden and graceful in the sun. "You see the rainbows?" Kathy said.

"They're catching rainbows?"

"No, silly, the rainbows in your eyelashes. I remember reading somewhere that if you close your eyes just enough but not too much, and the sun is just right, you can see rainbows."

I tried it, tightening my eyelids until they were completely shut, opening them and then trying again. "I don't see any rainbows," I said.

"They're there, I promise you. Try it again, more slowly this time."

I lowered my eyelids again, the sun high overhead, the rays warm on my face. And then I saw them, a whole line of rainbows shimmering on the ends of my eyelashes, and thought of the great bear framed for that one passing moment in that corona of rainbows we had seen only a day or two ago yet seeming like it all had happened in another lifetime. "I see them now," I said.

She wiggled a bit, settling her shoulders and head down onto me like a sleepy cat. I watched through the rainbows as Larry cast his line; graceful, strong, and beautiful. I would have drifted into what I'm sure would have been a delightful nap in the sun had not a distant, mechanical whine disturbed the solemn peace. A boat's motor, approaching fast. Civilization coming to reclaim us. I patted Kathy's sun-warmed hair. "Our ride's here."

Kathy yawned. "Tell them to come back in an hour," she said.

"I'm guessing that's not an option."

She yawned again and stretched, then slid an arm beneath me. "I could stay here forever." She clasped one hand in the other, squeezing me tightly in her encircling arms. "Could you stay here forever?"

"Absolutely."

"Liar." She freed her arm, stood up and took my hand. "We better get going before we're stranded."

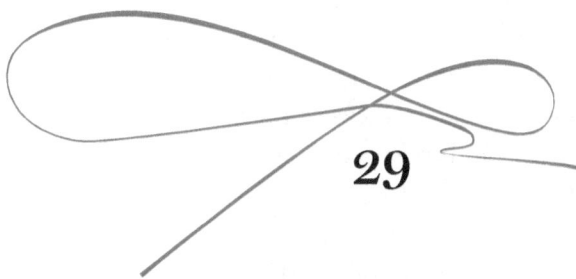

29

Billy welcomed our return to the Nalunaq Inn with a dinner of grilled moose steaks; garlic mashed potatoes; a tomato, cucumber, and onion salad; and ice cream smothered in fresh-picked Alaskan blueberries exploding in bursts of indescribable sweetness. Afterward, some of us headed out to take in the fireworks finale of the Nalunaq Delta State Fair. Exhausted, Wiley headed straight for his room.

It felt good to get out into the cool evening air, many of us slipping into the sweaters or hoodies we had taken with us, welcome warmth against the chill breeze that kicked up with the setting of the sun. Only a week ago, there still would have been daylight at this late hour. Here in the chill of the gloaming I could feel autumn rushing in, just as Wiley had foretold.

We walked down the short road that ended at the western point of the peninsula between the Kuskokwim and the Nalunaq, terminating at the massive earthen wall erected to protect the town from the annual spring floods on the ice-dammed rivers. Climbing the levee was not easy, our boots sank deep into the soft earth. About ten steps up and Babcock gave up. Breathing heavily, he headed back to the inn, Tony alongside as always.

We were among the last of the crowd to arrive, joining about one hundred others on the firm, flat top of the levee. More than half were children, most not yet teenagers; mixtures of Inuit and Caucasian, faces as radiant as the wisps of clouds aglow in the fading rays of a sun recently set. The children seemed as wild and free as the country in which they lived, as wild as their barking, white-eyed wolfdogs that took hold of sleeves and shirts and pants and wrestled the laughing children to the ground.

A glowing flame, a hiss, a shower of sparks trailing upward into the sky—the fireworks had begun. I don't know why these fireworks seemed to be the most beautiful I'd ever seen. Perhaps I didn't expect much, jaded by my occasional trip to the National Mall in Washington, D.C., on the Fourth to witness the fireworks extravaganza. Perhaps the beauty lay in seeing the whole show, from lighting to launch to dazzling climax—even to epilogue, when bits of fire fell back to earth, chased by packs of screaming children and their howling dogs along the mudflats. Perhaps because, out here, those small puffs of light, color, and sound seemed so incredibly trivial within the immeasurable immensity of the place and were not meant to be more so.

After a while, Larry said he was tired. He and Garrett headed back to the inn. "I guess I'll see you love birds back at the ranch," Zack said to Kathy and me not too long afterward. He bounded down the slope of the levee and disappeared into the night.

"Are we that obvious?" I said.

"I don't know, and I don't care." Kathy put her arms around my neck and drew me close for a kiss. "I thought I'd leave you my e-mail and phone number, in case you want to get in touch with me when we're back home. Do you Facebook?"

"No."

"Why did I even ask?" I got out my notebook, ripped out a sheet and handed it to her. "Too bad we've got roommates," Kathy said.

"Yeah. Too bad."

"There's always the riverbank." Down below, a few people worked in the glare of headlights from a couple of parked flatbeds to disassemble the fireworks launchers. "Maybe not," Kathy said. I laughed and kissed her. "You better call me," she whispered.

"You better answer."

We kissed again, a long, moonlit kiss alone atop the mound of earth protecting the fragile village. Kathy broke it off and sighed. "What?" I said.

"Those cubs. Every time I think about them, those pelts hanging down from the log next to their dead mother, it depresses me."

"The pelts are going to get those hunters busted. Wiley's already put in a call."

"That's something, at least."

"Can I ask you a question?" I said.

Her eyes fixed on mine. "Anything," she said.

"I was wondering—can you introduce me to John McPhee someday?"

"Seriously? *That's* what you wanted to ask me?"

"No, not really. Actually, I was wondering if your roommate might be planning to sleep elsewhere tonight."

"Unfortunately, no. Since it's our last night out here, Angie said she wanted to spend the night with me."

"Too bad."

Kathy smiled. "Rain check?" she said.

I squeezed her hand. We loped down the side of the levee and headed back to our rooms.

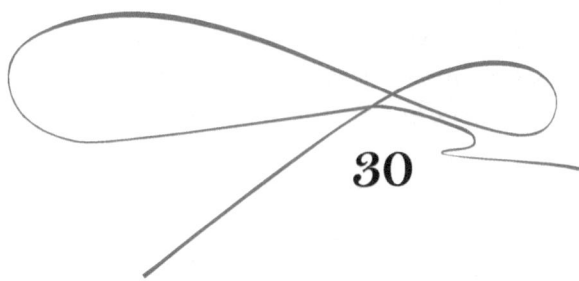

30

It was difficult to sleep with a solid roof overhead, absent the fresh chill of night air. The room felt stuffy, quiet. I could sense that Larry, too, was awake. "Can't sleep?" I said.

"I want to see the lights," Larry said. I heard him stir, leave his bed.

"I'll come with you."

We walked down the rutted, flood-lit road paralleling the runway outside the chain link fence, our footsteps crunching the gravel, our backs to the town, the levee, the convergence of the rivers. The fence ended. We continued on, the road now bounded by a stand of trees on the left, a dark, low curtain against the sky. I glanced up and it struck me that, beyond the poster taped to the wall in Larry's isolation room, I didn't really know what the northern lights looked like, or whether we could hope to see them in the light of a full moon. We stood together, scanning the sky, silent but for the uneven rhythm of our breathing. I guessed at the identity of the points of light I could see through the glare of the moonlight: Venus? Jupiter? Vega?

A flash of brilliant light flamed across the sky, blazing over the town and the river. "Holy shit, did you see that!" Larry said.

And then came the howling, as if every wolf hunting in the surrounding wilderness had seen it, too; plaintive howls all around us, one howl answered by another.

"We may not see any northern lights tonight, but that was something!" Larry said.

"Definitely."

"What do you say? Back to bed?"

"Good idea."

We headed back to the inn, Larry's arm draped across my shoulder.

*****

I sat by the window for the night-long flight home. I had intended to do some work reading on the way. I stared at the *Science* reprint on my fold-down tray—*Further Elucidation of the Caspase-associated Signaling Pathways Central to Programmed Cell Death in Peripheral Blood Mononuclear Cells; A Genomic and Proteomic Analysis*—unable to begin reading the abstract.

Larry saved me. They were showing the original *Men in Black* on the ceiling drop-down screens aboard this ancient plane. He suggested we watch it together. I put the document onto the floor, put on my headphones, and settled down with him to watch.

I watched a good part of it before my mind wandered to thoughts of Kathy. I turned away and stared out the window into the frigid blackness.

The movie ended. Larry slipped off his headphones and I did the same. He clicked on his overhead reading light, threw a handful of honey-roasted peanuts into his mouth, washed them down with the glass of Jack Daniels on ice he had sweet-talked the stewardess into giving him for free. "Good movie, huh?" he said, the woody smell of the whiskey sweet on his breath.

"Total classic."

"You can read your paper now," he said.

"Thanks. Right now, I don't feel much like a hot-shot scientist."

Larry swirled his glass, draining the remains of his whiskey. "I'll be damned," he said. "I think you're in love." I said nothing. "Kathy's pretty cool."

"Yes, she is."

"You got her number, right? E-mail? Address?"

"I got it."

"Good. Don't lose it." Larry yawned. "I'm going to get some sleep." He put his headphones back on against the engine noise, turned off the light, rolled over onto his side.

I turned once more to look out at the blackness of the night before pulling down the window-shade and drifting off to sleep.

Strange. A corner of the sky no longer seemed dark. We were traveling east. Moonrise? No moonrise I'd ever seen looked like this. It spread before my eyes, a green velvet curtain suspended across the heavens, subtly changing as if blown by a gentle wind.

"It's the lights!" I said as I shook Larry's shoulder.

"What the hell?"

"It's the *lights*, Larry! The *northern lights*!"

Larry's eyes widened. He pulled off his headphones and dove over me, peanuts spilling from the jostled tray table, cupping his hands around his eyes, his head pressed to the window. "Unbelievable! Bro, I need your seat!"

I slid beneath him, brushed off the loose peanuts from his seat, sat down. Larry's face remained plastered against the window, my head resting upon his broad, strong shoulder, watching until the heavenly glow faded into the brightness of the coming day.

ACKNOWLEDGMENTS

A familiar refrain but worth repeating: Writing a book is never a solitary endeavor. Along the way, I've been fortunate to have the support, guidance, and encouragement of many talented individuals.

Sincere thanks to:

Jacqueline Salmon, for guiding me through the publishing wilderness and pulling together an enjoyable and talented team to assist. Amy Foster for her artistic talent in creating the cover design.

The Johns Hopkins University Master's program in Writing (fiction concentration) and my talented and insightful instructors. Special appreciation to Richard Peabody (the first to tell me that I had the "chops" to be a writer); Claire Messud, whose class I was fortunate to take during her time as a visiting writer/lecturer; Tim Wendel; and Bill Loizeaux.

Literary agent Laura Strachan, who believed in this story enough to inspire me to chart a new path toward bringing it to life. Editor Leslie Wells, and novelist and friend Lori Banov Kaufmann, for their insightful guidance.

Pamela Rossi and Katerina Chapman for their close reading of the manuscript, valuable and encouraging comments, and friendship—and Pam for her meticulous proofreading.

The Kauai Writer's Conference and associated instructors, including Téa Obreht, Nicholas Delbanco, and Joshua Mohr, for providing invaluable insights into the creative process.

Alice McDermott, Bethesda, Maryland's gift to the literary world, for teaching me that at the beating heart of literary novels lay an exploration of "life, love, and death."

The late John Gardner for writing *The Art of Fiction*, my literary lodestar from the first time I picked up a pen (yes, that long ago) and attempted to write fiction. The late Professor Laurence Holland, former chairman of the English Department at Johns Hopkins University, whose Gilman Hall lectures, presented with a gravelly voice and eyes glancing over his pince—nez, guided me into hidden dimensions of classic novels I never would have discovered on my own.

Deb, Josh, and Ben, for their love and support.

My closest friends, Mike, Les, Sheldon, Dee, Yadin, and Craig, for keeping me semi-sane and smiling and for pushing me to put my work into the public eye, even when the journey wasn't easy.

My late parents, Alvin and Gloria, who encouraged me to use my imagination in whatever I chose to do.

Frances, Elana, and Alec, the best, most loving and supportive family I could ever hope for.

And to my late brother, Ralph—physician, sportsman, loving husband and father, and loyal friend—who, when he wasn't saving the lives of premature babies, was tying some of the most radically radiant fishing flies cast on America's pristine rivers.